7

The Finches' Fabulous Furnace

Roger Drury

Inside illustrations by Erik Blegvad

AN
APPLE
PAPERBACK

SCHOLASTIC INC.
New York Toronto London Auckland Sydney

for Julie
with her father's thanks
for persuading him to turn this wild story loose

ISBN 0-590-42448-3

Text copyright © 1971 by Roger W. Drury. Inside illustrations copyright © 1971 by Erik Blegvad. All rights reserved. Published by Scholastic Inc., 730 Broadway, New York, NY 10003, by arrangement with Little Brown & Company, Inc. APPLE PAPERBACKS is a registered trademark of Scholastic Inc.

12 11 10 9 8 7 6 5 4   2 3 4/9

The Finches' Fabulous Furnace

1

Peter Finch felt like a giant. By standing close against the model of Ashfield and reaching his arms right and left, he could touch both ends of town. He leaned forward and blew at the tiny gilded weathervane on top of the church steeple. It spun wildly for a moment, then came to a stop, pointing at him and trembling on its pivot.

The model looked so real, with bright green grass around the houses, he could almost forget the snow coming down outside where Mrs. Finch and Patsy were waiting in the car. They must be wondering what kept him and his father so long.

Across the room, Mr. Finch was talking to the real estate agent about renting a house. There seemed to be some big difficulty.

"I don't believe it," Mr. Finch was saying. "I know you didn't expect us before the first of the year, but surely you know of some other house in Ashfield that would suit our needs. What about the one we had for our vacation here two years ago?"

Peter's eyes traveled over the model. Three blocks down from Trask's Grocery, turn left half a block and there it was, tiny as a peanut, the house they had lived in that August, when he was eight and Mrs. Finch's hay fever was so bad.

"Try Ashfield," the doctor back home in New Jersey had advised. And he was right. Once they were in Ashfield, her hay fever had stopped and she felt fine.

Now Ambrose Marveldale was explaining to Mr. Finch that none of the summer cottages would do for a year-round house because they had no central heating or insulation.

"The only suitable houses," he said, shaking his head regretfully, "have been taken in the last few weeks. It's all because of our new baby powder factory, of course. You're not the only one coming to a job there." He tilted way back in his leather desk chair and frowned. "Have you thought of looking in Hampton? It's not far — maybe six miles down in the valley."

"Might as well be six hundred," Mr. Finch said, "if it isn't Ashfield. Ever since our summer here, I've been looking for a job in this area — just so Mrs. Finch can live in Ashfield. Now I have the job and we've come, but — no house!"

Peter had never heard his father so discouraged. Through the wide front window of the real estate office, on which MARVELDALE was painted backwards in fancy black and gold letters, he saw the snow coming down more heavily than before among the twisting branches of the trees. He crossed the office and perched on the arm of his father's chair.

"And what can we do tonight?" Mr. Finch added. "We expected to stay in a motel for a few days until our furniture came, but every motel we passed was jammed with cars. NO VACANCY."

"Skiers," Ambrose Marveldale explained, waving one hand towards the window behind him. "It's this early snow, coming on a weekend. We're getting to be as famous for skiers in the winter as we are for sneezers in summer. They fill up the motels and the spare rooms — everything."

"Then you really can't help us? There's nothing in Ashfield? Not even for tonight?"

"Nothing at all! That is — " Mr. Marveldale pulled out a drawer an inch or two and pushed it shut again — "that is, nothing you'd care for."

"Then you do have something!" exclaimed Mr. Finch. "But why do you think we wouldn't like it?"

Mr. Marveldale fidgeted with his fountain pen. "I shouldn't have mentioned it. It's been vacant for more than a year. You see, it just isn't s-suitable to live in."

"Why not?" Mr. Finch persisted. "Does the roof

leak? Is it too small? Chimney cracked? Termites?"

"Maybe it has ghosts," Peter said hopefully.

"No, not ghosts! Of course there were rumors — some of the neighbors did wonder why the last people — the Jarvises — left so suddenly, before the end of their lease. Would you mind a house if people said it had ghosts, Peter?"

"I'd like to see a real one and find out if they can go through walls — things like that. If one tried to scare me, I'd shoot a blowtorch at it and make it evaporate."

"Dry it up, eh?" The smile faded from Mr. Marveldale's round face. He looked at Peter's father again, solemnly.

"I wonder . . ." He tapped his fingertips together. "It's possible — just possible — there's really nothing else. A young family like yours. Perhaps . . . could I talk to you alone for a few minutes?"

Mr. Finch motioned towards Peter with his head. "This young man is pretty grown-up about keeping secrets," he said.

"Oh, I'm sure he is — undoubtedly," Mr. Marveldale agreed. "Only . . . I'd prefer to talk to you alone."

"Tell you what, Pete," Mr. Finch said. "You go down and see if Mum and Patsy are getting impatient. Say I won't be much longer. I hope I won't."

After Peter went out, Ambrose Marveldale seemed more nervous than before. He stood up, walked around his desk two or three times, then went to the window and stared out at the falling snow. It was beginning to be twilight.

"This house you were talking about — " Mr. Finch said. "What would the rent be?"

"Oh, the rent!" The real estate agent sat down at his desk again. "The rent would be low — very low. In fact — if you agreed — I should be happy . . ." He seemed to be having trouble finishing his sentences and his eyes were vague, as if they looked through Mr. Finch and out the other side, at something far off.

"Somebody ought to be there," he said, half to himself, "keeping an eye on the place. But of course," he added, and now he really was looking at Mr. Finch, "you would have to agree — you would have to promise . . . . Can you keep all this under your hat, eh?"

Mr. Finch was uneasy. "If there's nothing illegal about it," he said. "You aren't printing counterfeit money in the cellar there, I hope?"

"Dear me, no!" The real estate man laughed nervously. "I should hope not! It's true that the cellar of Number Seven, Pride Street, is unusual. A very peculiar cellar. But not another word unless you promise to keep it a secret."

"Of course I do. Of course!" Mr. Finch had lost patience. He could see no reason for all this mystery.

"Well then," said Ambrose Marveldale, taking a deep breath, "I will tell you. The Jarvises left because of a smell — a really sickening odor like rotten eggs —

9

that began to come up through a crack in the cellar floor."

"That doesn't sound too bad. It could be cemented over."

"If there was nothing else," Ambrose Marveldale said in a low voice. "But the smell was only a beginning. For fifteen months now, I've kept the place off the market while I tried to make up my mind what to do."

"Yes, yes," exploded Mr. Finch, "but look!" He pointed to the window. "It's nearly dark. Four o'clock in the evening. December. My wife and children are outside, waiting in the car. Can't you come to the point? What is wrong with that house?" He slapped the edge of the desk with his hand.

Mr. Marveldale sighed. "Come to the point, yes," he said. "Well, sir, the only drawback to Number Seven, Pride Street — and otherwise it's a beautiful property, in a nice neighborhood; well built, clean, fine lawn, shade trees — everything you could ask for, and furnished besides — the only drawback is that in the cellar there's a small volcano."

2

"A what!" said the startled Mr. Finch. "Did you say a volcano?"

"A small one, you understand," Mr. Marveldale hurried to repeat. "It's been there since a week after the Jarvises left. Small. Not very violent. Some steam. Hot, yes, but no lava. At least," he hesitated, "at least not when I saw it last."

"When was that?" demanded Mr. Finch.

Ambrose Marveldale cleared his throat. He pulled at his lower lip.

"When? Let me see. It was — um — it was about the end of June, I think. Yes, the last Sunday in June. Just before the summer people began arriving in town."

"And you've left this — volcano — unwatched all that time?" Mr. Finch asked unbelievingly. "Why, the house could be full of ashes and rocks. It could have burned down!"

"Well, I must say I was worried at first," Ambrose Marveldale said. "I checked up on it every Sunday morning on my way to church. But it was always the same, so I've been easier in my mind about it lately. Still, whenever I go by the house, I make sure there's no steam leaking out of windows, you know — that sort of thing. But it always looks calm and peaceful."

"But the neighbors? How do they feel, living next door to a house that has a volcano in the cellar?"

"Oh, I didn't — I haven't — I mean, they don't —"

Mr. Finch's eyes opened wide. "You mean they don't *know*?"

"Well, if they did, do you honestly think they'd believe it? Who ever heard of a volcano in New England? I mean, nowadays? I couldn't believe it myself at first. Then, by the time I was sure it really was a volcano, I was getting — oh, *used* to it, you know. And, as I said, it's been very well behaved.

"There's no more smell to it. For all we know, it may stay quiet for years and years. Why start a panic now? And yet — " Mr. Marveldale picked with his thumbnail at the edge of his desk — "I just didn't dare rent the house to anyone. Or tear it down, either. So there it is."

Mr. Finch looked towards the window again. Evening was falling over the bleak branches of trees along the street. It was still snowing.

"Let me have the key," he said. "I think we can risk it for one night. We'll look the place over, and perhaps I'll be back in the morning to discuss a lease. It may not be as dangerous as it sounds."

The Finches' car made its way from Ambrose Marveldale's office to Pride Street in only a few minutes. Mr. Finch drove slowly up the street while Mrs. Finch peered out, looking for numbers on the lighted porches.

"Sixteen, fourteen," she said. "Twelve, ten. It must be on the other side. Maybe that one with no lights. My, it's a big one! Is that Number Seven?"

The minute the car stopped, Peter was out of it first and running up the path of the big dark house.

"This is it, Pop," he called back. "Number Seven."

"Oh, Daddy," Patsy said, "what a wonderful place to play in!"

"But, Harry," gasped Mrs. Finch, "can we ever keep up with the rent on such a house?"

Number Seven was big; no doubt of that. As far as they could see in the dark, it was the most imposing house on that side of Pride Street. It was white and three stories high, with a round tower at each front corner — like oatmeal boxes with Chinese hats, Patsy said — and a wide lawn all around; an old-fashioned sort of house, needing new paint, but sturdy and welcoming.

Would Mr. Marveldale mind if he shared the secret with his wife? Mr. Finch wondered. But tonight would be a bad time for it. She would only be alarmed and lose sleep.

"Never mind about the rent," he reassured her. "First, let's see how the house is inside. Marveldale said we could spend a night here before making up our minds. It'll be damp and chilly, maybe, because the furnace has been shut off since June. Still, we're lucky to get anything."

The door opened easily and a draft of warm air met them as they stepped in.

"Thank goodness it's heated after all!" Mrs. Finch exclaimed. "Now if the lights work . . ." She tried a switch near the door, which immediately filled the large hallway with a cheerful glow. "See! Now all we need is some supper!"

Mr. Finch glanced quickly around. There was no sign of ash on the floor — only the light coating of dust one would expect after a house had been closed for over a year.

Before the others had their coats off, Mrs. Finch had found the kitchen. In one corner there was a door ajar, opening to a stairway going down.

"These must be the cellar stairs, Harry," she called

over her shoulder. "Just feel the heat coming up! My, isn't that nice on a raw day like this."

"Certainly is, yes," mumbled Mr. Finch. "But I'll bet it's dusty as anything down there. Why don't you inspect the kitchen — see if we have the makings of supper with us — while I go down and take a look. Kids, you might explore upstairs. There are rooms enough so each of you can choose your own."

Peter and Patsy made a dash for the hall. Mr. Finch waited until he heard the wide front stairs booming under their feet. Then he turned, gulped, and started down into the cellar.

3

"Food first, then talk!" Mrs. Finch said. "It's been a long day and we're all tired. So eat your toast while it's hot, everybody. After that, all of us can report what we found and how we like the house."

Mr. Finch needed time to think. How should he tell the family what he had seen in the cellar? Or how could he keep it secret? He helped himself to several pieces of toast and plenty of marmalade and butter and settled down to keep busy eating, as long as possible.

Peter was rushing to be finished first, but he was still chewing on a mouthful of toast and peanut butter when Patsy put in her last bite. He chewed faster.

"Can I — " his tongue struggled to get out of the

peanut butter, "can I have the round room?"

"I think we ought to hear from Daddy first," Mrs. Finch said. "When he's ready."

"Oh no," Mr. Finch said. "I'm in no hurry. But swallow, Peter, before you begin."

Then Patsy burst in and began to tell about the wonderful top floor, "up two sets of stairs," and the room with the chimney in the middle and dormer windows looking out in four different directions.

Peter was sure he had found something even better in his exploration of the second floor — the round rooms in the corner towers. He begged to be allowed to have one of them.

"It'll be like living in a lighthouse," he said.

"And you, my dear," Mr. Finch asked, as he buttered another piece of toast, "how do you like the kitchen?"

Mrs. Finch smiled, closed her eyes, and opened them again.

"It's a dream," she said. "Gas range, big refrigerator, double sink, endless cupboards — everything. Not too big; not too small; easy to keep clean. And it's been kept so clean! In fact, except for a little dust, the whole house is spotless. The last people here — she must have been a wonderful housekeeper. But it's such a big house! I do hope we can afford the rent. Were you pleased with the furnace, Harry? It must be a good one."

"What?" Mr. Finch swallowed hard. "Oh yes, I think the house will keep very comfortable. Maybe too warm sometimes."

"That's better than not warm enough," Mrs. Finch remarked. "What kind is it?"

"What kind is what?"

"The furnace. What kind is it?"

"Oh, it's a — it's a volcano," said Mr. Finch.

"Never heard of that," Mrs. Finch said. "There are just too many makes nowadays to keep up with. I hope it's dependable, that's all."

"So do I," said Mr. Finch. "So do I."

4

The whole family slept like logs that night, Patsy under the roof in her chimney room with the four dormer windows, Peter on the third floor in his lighthouse, and Mr. and Mrs. Finch in a big square room opposite the head of the stairs.

Near dawn, Mr. Finch woke up. The house was absolutely still. Mrs. Finch was sound asleep. Was he crazy to let her and the children spend a night in this house? Or was it possible they could go on staying here safely?

He thought he would never get back to sleep. Although there was a window wide open, the room seemed terribly stuffy and hot. He pushed back the covers. Maybe he ought to wake Mrs. Finch and tell her — or would it be better not to tell anyone? Finally he must have dozed off, because suddenly —

"Wake up, wake up, Daddy," he heard Patsy's voice calling him. "There's a robin on the lawn and Mummy has breakfast almost—"

"Robin on the lawn? Nonsense, Patsy. It's December. There couldn't be."

"There is, though. Anyway, everybody else is up. Mummy has breakfast almost ready and Peter's ex-

ploring the cellar and — Daddy! What's the matter?"

Mr. Finch was halfway downstairs before Patsy could turn around. Across the kitchen he bounded, through the door to the cellar stairs and down them three steps at a time.

Peter was sitting on the bottom step.

"What's your hurry, Dad?" he said. "It isn't erupting. It *is* a volcano, isn't it?"

"Yes, it is, Peter, but shhh,'" implored Mr. Finch. "Let's not tell the whole world about it. There's no need to upset Mummy and Pat. If you and I use our heads, I'm sure we can work out a way to make it safe enough to live here. And we'd better; there isn't another vacant house in town."

Mr. Finch sat down on the bottom step beside Peter with his elbows on his knees and his chin in his hands and stared at the neat little hill of blackish-gray material in the middle of the cellar. A collar of broken concrete chunks surrounded it, pushed back when it had burst through the floor. From a hole in the top, wisps of steam floated out and vanished.

"I hoped it would turn out that Ambrose Marveldale was wrong," Mr. Finch said; "maybe what he called a volcano was only a mud pie made by one of the Jarvis children. But look at that! Feel it! No wonder it was hot upstairs last night!"

"And listen to it," Peter said. "If you're very quiet, you can hear it keep going 'glug, glug' down deep inside. It's like somebody gargling molasses."

"Just let it stay down deep, that's all I hope," said Mr. Finch.

"We could stick a whistle in the top," Peter suggested. "Then it'll blow its own alarm if it gets up too much steam. And golly, Pop, what a swell incinerator it'll be — and for toasting marshmallows! Boy, I can think of lots of things we can do with it. I bet there's nobody else in the whole world that has their own pet Vesuvius!"

"Shhh, Peter, please! Somehow, you and I are going to have to keep this a secret."

"Wow!" said Peter. "What a secret! A v— in the cellar!"

"Peter and I have been looking over the heating system," Mr. Finch said, as they returned to the kitchen.

"In your pajamas, Henry?" laughed Mrs. Finch. "You went through here as if you were on your way to a fire!"

"Yes; well, I didn't want Peter getting himself into any kind of trouble. In fact, we've decided it will be best to keep this door at the top of the stairs locked."

"Is the furnace unsafe?" asked Mrs. Finch. "Isn't it a reliable manufacturer?"

Peter winked at his father.

"I didn't mean that," Mr. Finch said. "It's quite

new, as a matter of fact. Only, the stairs are steep and — it's better not to play around down there. Besides, there's a good deal of fine dust that might get stirred up. You know what it does to your nose!"

Mrs. Finch frowned. "In that case," she said, "I'll gladly leave the cellar to you menfolks."

Breakfast was soon over. Peter and Patsy wanted to see the upstairs rooms by daylight, and Mrs. Finch wanted to ask some questions.

"It's all perfect," she said to her husband, "except for one thing. I can't understand why you let Mr. Marblegale persuade you to look at a house as big as this. It must cost a fortune to heat! And I hate to guess what the rent would be."

"Oh, Marveldale didn't have to persuade me," Mr. Finch said. "I was the one who did the persuading. As soon as I heard this was the only place in town, I jumped at it."

"But to heat it — three stories? Won't it cost us a fortune?"

Mr. Finch smiled. "No, my dear. Unless I miss my guess, that volcano down there is going to give us the cheapest winter heat we ever had."

"I wish," said Mrs. Finch, "you'd stop calling it a volcano. It makes me nervous. And what about the rent?"

"The rent may be another pleasant surprise," Mr. Finch said. "And that reminds me. Before Ambrose

Marveldale changes his mind, I'd better get over to his office and see about signing a lease."

It had just started to snow again. The air was thick with whirling flakes as Mr. Finch got out of his car at Mr. Marveldale's office. When he came out, he found snow plastered on the windshield and piled thick all over the car, but when he walked up the path at Number Seven, Pride Street, with a copy of the lease in his pocket and a book in his hand which he had stopped to pick up at the town library, he was astonished to see that the snowflakes melted instantly as they touched the ground near the house. And Patsy had been right: There was a robin hopping this way and that on the grass. As he watched, the robin jabbed the sod with its beak and pulled out a wriggling worm.

Mrs. Finch was waiting anxiously for him in the hall.

"Well," she asked, "what did he say?"

For answer, her husband handed her the lease.

"Read this," he said. The document was very short:

In consideration of the sum of one (1) dollar, paid to me by Henry Finch, I, Ambrose Marveldale, do hereby lease the premises at Number Seven, Pride Street, to the aforesaid Finch for a period of three (3) years from this date, with the stipulation that he assumes all risks and responsi-

*bilities of said tenancy and will never at any time
divulge the terms of this agreement.*

"How much is the rent?" Mrs. Finch asked, looking
up from the paper. "And what was the dollar for?"

"Don't you see?" said Mr. Finch. "That one dollar
is the rent."

"One dollar?" Mrs. Finch whispered. "For three
years? I feel dizzy." She put her hand over her eyes.

The library book dropped from Mr. Finch's hand
as he reached out to steady her. But he was too late.
Right there on the hall rug, with the lease still in her
hand, she fainted dead away.

5

So the Finches were going to stay at Number Seven. It was all settled. Almost. Mrs. Finch would not have dreamed of saying no to such a bargain, yet she knew very well there was something queer about the place. If there wasn't, she kept saying to herself, why would Mr. Marblegale be practically paying them to live there? But she was so happy over the kitchen and the extra rooms upstairs, where Peter and Patsy could play on bad days without being in her way, that she asked Mr. Finch no more questions.

On Sunday, he visited the cellar several times, "to check on the furnace," he said. He did seem strangely nervous about it, Mrs. Finch thought, but if his worry had anything to do with the low rent she didn't find out what it was. And he spent at least an hour in the afternoon hunting high and low through the house, mostly in the front hall, as if he had lost something.

"Oh, don't worry," he said when she offered to help.

"It's nothing. I'll find it. I must have put it down somewhere else."

On Monday morning, he made her promise to call up Ambrose Marveldale if anything in the house went out of order during the day. Then he got in the car and started off to his new job at the baby powder factory.

Peter and Patsy left for school half an hour later. The Ashfield Center School was less than three blocks from Pride Street and they found they could walk there easily in five minutes. It was an old building, much smaller than the school they had been attending back in New Jersey.

They separated in the corridor. In the sixth grade room every desk was filled, but an extra chair with a wide arm to write on had been placed for Peter at the back. He scrambled into it just as the bell rang.

A boy with carrot-colored hair, who sat just in front of him, lost no time in striking up an acquaintance. As soon as the teacher was looking away, he balanced a folded note on his thumbnail and flipped it neatly over his shoulder. It landed right in Peter's lap.

Are you from the Spooky House? it said.

Peter wrote at the bottom, *Number Seven, Pride Street. What's your name?* folded it and pushed it with his foot to a place where carrot-head could reach it.

At that point, the teacher interrupted the boys' exchange by calling Peter to her desk for books and paper, and to be introduced to the class. But as soon as he was back in his seat another note dropped into his lap.

That's the Spooky House all right. I'm Red Pitcher. It's haunted.

Class discussion of the exports of Costa Rica now halted the penciled conversation and forced the boys to wait until recess.

"Hey, have you seen any ghosts yet?" Red wanted to know right off.

"Who says the house has ghosts?" demanded Peter. "If I see one, I'll throw a glass of water in his face! What makes you think there're ghosts there anyway?"

"I've seen 'em. Once I was going by just before dark, and saw 'em sliding out the cellar window."

"Yeah," put in another boy. "I saw one, too, just like that, coming out the cellar window, long and twisty. Started off across the grass, and then — poof! — it disappeared. Vanished, just like they do in scary books!"

Patsy had joined the group around Peter and was listening, her eyes wide. Was this teasing, or truth?

"Gee, I wouldn't want to live in that place," said the carrot-head. "Remember what happened to Jumpy Jarvis? Came to Little League practice one day all white 'n' jumpier than ever. Said they had something weird in the cellar. I remember just what Jumpy said

too. 'You can't see anything, but you can smell it all right, and it *hisses*.' Boy, I wouldn't live in that place if you paid me a million bucks!"

There was quite a crowd of listeners by now. It began to look to Peter as if merely living in the Spooky House would make a hero of him.

"And just a couple of days later," Red went on, "Jumpy's family got in their car and drove away and never came back."

"What does this ghost look like?" Peter asked. "I mean, what color was it when you saw it? How was it dressed?"

"How was it dressed? Wow!" exclaimed Red. "You think I waited around to see if it had suspenders on? Or a hoop skirt? Or a tall hat like Abraham Lincoln? All I know is, it was sort of fog-color."

"Me too," said the other boy who claimed to have seen the ghost. "Fog-color and thin. I could see the shingles on the side of the house right through it."

Peter shrugged his shoulders.

"Well," he said, "maybe I've seen it already, then."

"You *have*? Gee, what did you do? Yell at it? Did it hiss at you like it did at Jumpy? Did it wave its arms? Were you scared?" The questions came all at once.

Patsy stared at her brother. What would he say next?

"Oh sure," Peter laughed. "It hissed all right. And I guess it hadn't any bones, 'cause it waved all over like a flag. But I saw it wasn't gonna come after me, so I just sat down and watched it."

"You sat down and watched it! I believe that! Oh, I believe every word of that! You sat down and made yourself comfortable and just watched it, did you? How long?"

"Oh, about ten minutes, I guess," said Peter. "But if you don't believe me —"

The bell rang. As they went to their rooms again, Patsy whispered to Peter, "What did you say those things for? You haven't seen any ghost. Have you?"

"Sh," said Peter. "It's a secret."

"What's a secret?"

"What I saw."

"Then it wasn't a ghost?"

"That's the secret."

6

About the middle of the morning, the moving van arrived from New Jersey with the Finches' chairs and rugs and dishes and books and blankets and extra clothes; and Peter's kites and bicycle; and Patsy's puppet stage and box of puppets; and everything else.

Especially the vacuum cleaner. That was what Mrs. Finch had been waiting for. As soon as the moving men had left, she carried it up to Patsy's room on the top floor, tied on the dust mask she always wore while cleaning, and began.

Though the house was certainly big, it turned out to be fairly easy to clean. Mrs. Finch skipped the bedrooms they were not using on the second floor, but went systematically through all the others, and by the end of the morning most of the house had the look and feel of fresh cleanness which her tidy nature liked.

She did the front hall last. The end of the vacuum cleaner caught on something under the umbrella stand and hooked it out onto the rug. A book. It was stamped in gold letters on the cover, ASHFIELD FREE TOWN LIBRARY.

Mrs. Finch dusted off the book and carried it with her to the kitchen, where she made herself a light lunch and sat down with a sigh of relief. The silence was delicious after the roar of the vacuum cleaner all morning. Of course, the house wasn't all clean yet. The windows would have to be done next, and the curtains would need a washing.

She opened the library book. Pictures of mountains. The Grand Canyon. Diagrams of the earth, cut in half like an orange. She flipped the pages back to the beginning. *The Landscape and How It Grew,* was the title. She sipped her coffee while one hand turned the pages.

About halfway through, a scrap of paper was stuck in, marking the start of a chapter on volcanoes.

Volcanoes again! There were several pages about the famous eruptions — Vesuvius, Etna, Pelée, Krakatoa. Her eye was caught by a long paragraph which told how the new volcano, Paricutín, had burst out of a farmer's cornfield in Mexico just a few years ago. There was a photograph of it, now hundreds of feet high. Further on were photographs of Pompeii, buried alive by the eruption of Vesuvius.

Mrs. Finch shuddered. Imagine naming a furnace a Volcano! Why would any furnace maker want to do that? Because it was hot? Maybe. But all these other thoughts that the word brought to her mind — danger, violence, destruction, explosions — what about them? No, if she were advertising a furnace, she would certainly never call it a Volcano.

The house was amazingly quiet with the children away at school. Mrs. Finch always felt a little deaf for an hour or so after vacuuming. But really, there was no sound at all, except a faint hum from the kettle on the range. Even the furnace made no sound. Come to think of it, she hadn't heard it turn on at all while she was eating lunch.

That was odd, because it was cold outdoors, with a wind. She listened intently. Not a murmur. And yet the house was wonderfully warm; really too warm, especially here in the kitchen. Somewhere there must be a thermostat. Perhaps she ought to set it several degrees lower.

After a few minutes' search, she found the thermostat in a corner of the hallway. To her astonishment, it was already set as low as it would go — about forty degrees.

Mrs. Finch's thoughts began to whirl. With the thermostat dial turned down to forty, the furnace shouldn't be running at all. Yet the house was very warm — the thermometer said eighty — so the furnace was certainly putting out heat. Maybe it was staying on, even when it was supposed to shut off. It might be very dangerous.

She decided she had better telephone Mr. Barglepale. Right away. She almost ran to the telephone. The directory hanging beside it was small and thin. She quickly found Ashfield and ran her finger down the B's.

There was no Barglepale. What? No Barglepale? There must be! Did she have Ashfield? Yes. But there was no one listed by the name of Barglepale. Was that the right name? Heavens, the house was hot! Or was it Beagletail? Or Burglejail?

A knock sounded on the front door; a quiet, confident knock. Maybe it was the agent himself, come to see how they were getting along! Hoping it might be so, Mrs. Finch opened the door so suddenly that the plump woman on the doorstep exclaimed, "Oh!" and looked ready to turn around and run.

"I didn't mean to startle you," said Mrs. Finch. "Won't you come in?"

The plump woman hesitated. "Well, I..." she began, and peered beyond Mrs. Finch into the hallway as if to make sure there was no dangerous beast lurking in the shadows. Then she seemed satisfied and went on, "I came over to welcome you. I'm Alice

Pratt. Live in the next place but one, down that way, on this side." She gestured with a tilt of her head.

"Do come in," Mrs. Finch urged the visitor. "We're not settled yet, but the house has its own furniture, so at least I can offer you a place to sit down. Do come in."

Alice Pratt looked nervously about her as she entered and sniffed two or three times as if she had a runny nose and had forgotten her handkerchief.

"You found it heated, I'll wager," she said. "Well heated!"

"Why, yes," said Mrs. Finch. "Luckily it was. But how did you know? It's been empty, I thought, for over a year."

"I'll tell you how," the visitor smiled. "In the winter after Beth Jarvis and her family moved away, I never saw a particle of snow stay on this roof. Not a flake. No icicles, either — never. And I expect you've noticed the grass is growing outside there right now, as if it was June." She finished removing her overshoes and straightened up. "Now that's what I call heating a house!" she said. "And when it's an empty house, people can't be blamed for wondering why."

7

Wait till Harry hears that, Mrs. Finch thought, as she led her visitor into the living room.

"You mean while the house was empty, it was still heated enough to keep the grass growing around it, even in winter?" she asked.

"Yes, I do," said Alice Pratt; "with robins pulling worms in January, and never any oil truck coming that anybody saw, either, unless in the middle of the night, and nobody delivers oil at hours like that."

"Maybe it was heated some other way," Mrs. Finch suggested. "Gas — or coal?"

"In Ashfield? Not a chance! Town meeting put a ban on coal burners years ago. As for gas, the nearest pipeline must be a hundred miles away. Mind you, I don't believe in listening to gossip, but Amy Straw said she'd heard that one of Tinker Jarvis' machines had gone wild. Something that made a lot of heat out of a drop or two of oil. But there was a smell from it so awful they had to get out. Before their lease was up too. I notice there's no smell now, but it seems there was then, and they say Mrs. Jarvis couldn't stand it."

"Well, she certainly left the house neat and clean," Mrs. Finch remarked.

"Did she now? Cleaned it before she left! My, my!" said the visitor. "It was Mister who was the strange one, anyway. Tinker, they called him. A sort of inventor, you know. Spent most of his time working at machines and inventions, I heard, and when he was done with 'em, like as not they'd be too complicated to work. So they said. That rumor about a heat machine — I wonder if that was just a story."

The visitor paused. Mrs. Finch said nothing. She was thinking about her husband's frequent visits to the cellar the day before.

"Maybe," Alice Pratt prompted her, "you've noticed some odd attachment on the furnace?"

"No," said Mrs. Finch, "I — "

"Nothing at all unusual?" Alice Pratt insisted. "But there must be something."

"I was starting to say," Mrs. Finch began again, "that I haven't seen the furnace yet, or the cellar either. There's been enough to keep me busy without that."

"Well, surely your husband has been down there," the visitor said. "Didn't he say anything about the furnace?"

What an inquisitive neighbor she is, thought Mrs. Finch. Whatever I tell her, I'm sure she will gossip it all over Ashfield. Still, one must try to be polite.

"Harry did say our fuel bill will be low," she said. "And that will certainly be a blessing, won't it? Have you lived in Ashfield all your life?"

"All my life, yes; all my life," said Alice Pratt. "I'm one of those 'natives' you hear about and I suppose I know just about everyone in town. Seen a lot of comings and goings too. It brightens things up to have nice young newcomers like you here. This new factory — it's brought in five or six families. There's really quite a bustle here now, for a quiet old town like Ashfield. You've heard we're having our two hundredth anniversary in July?" 'Bicentennial,' they call it. A big celebration it'll be. Most everyone in Ashfield's on one of the committees. You'll be asked. I'll see to that."

"I'll be glad to help as much as I can," Mrs. Finch murmured.

"Pringle. A. J. Pringle — he's manager at the factory; owns it too — when they were laying the foundations last April, he came to the selectmen. 'How do you plan to celebrate the anniversary next year?' he said. 'What anniversary?' they asked him. That's how quiet Ashfield was — they didn't know there *was* any anniversary. Nobody did, except Calvin Starch — he's the librarian. He keeps track of all that sort of thing, and he'd got talking to A. J. Pringle about it. Pringle, he's what you call a live wire — too live for me, but he gets things done. Anyway, if it wasn't for him Ashfield would never have been all steamed up to celebrate this Bicentennial. So your husband thinks the furnace won't use much oil?"

Mrs. Finch was caught off guard. "Almost none," she said.

Alice Pratt fanned her neck with her pocketbook.

"Well, it's surely on the job today," she said. "That Jarvis was a clever fellow, right enough, but I never heard of getting heat without burning something." She looked at Mrs. Finch sideways, as if she thought a secret were being kept from her which she had a right to know.

"Maybe your husband expects the oil bill to be low," she went on, "but by the look of things, and the feel of things, there's a precious lot of something being burned at Number Seven, Pride Street, right now!"

The front door banged and children's voices resounded in the hall. "Yes, I *am* going to tell her," Patsy could be heard to say. Then, in Peter's voice, "No, you mustn't. Whose overshoes are those? There must be company."

"I don't care; I'm going to, anyway," Patsy's voice declared, and the next moment she came tumbling into the room.

"Mummy," she cried, ignoring the visitor, "Mummy, Peter told the kids at school he'd seen a ghost, here, in this house! It isn't true, is it?"

"Patsy, this is our neighbor, Miss Pratt," said Mrs. Finch. "And here is Peter," she added, as the boy made his slower entrance. "Let's save Peter and his ghost until supper. We mustn't bore Miss Pratt with that kind of foolishness."

"Oh, not at all," said the visitor. "If there are ghosts in town, I'd like to hear about it. Where did you see it, Peter?"

Peter kicked one foot against the other. "In the cellar," he mumbled. "But I didn't say it was a ghost. *They* did. And anyway . . ." He was silent again.

"A furnace that burns no oil, *and* a ghost! My!" exclaimed Miss Pratt. "I'd like to see a cellar like that."

"You can't. Daddy locked the door," Patsy said.

"Patsy, Peter, you run along now," said their mother hurriedly, and she hustled them out of the room.

"I must be going, anyway," Miss Pratt said. "You'll be full of questions about their first day at school, and I've several stops to make before I go home."

She bundled into her coat and overshoes and said good-bye to Mrs. Finch, and "See you soon." Down the path she went.

For about ten feet from the house, the grass was green. Then, for another five feet, it looked frozen, but still it was bare of snow. And after that, Alice Pratt walked in snow. The whole town was white except for Number Seven, Pride Street. She muttered as she walked, "So Daddy locked the cellar door? I wonder why."

"Don't you worry about the furnace," Mr. Finch told his wife that evening. "If it gets too hot in the house, just open a few windows. This kind can't be turned on and off like an ordinary furnace; the thermostat isn't even connected to it. And anyway," he laughed, "who ever heard of putting a thermostat on a volcano?"

"Oh, you joker!" said Mrs. Finch. "All right, then, I won't worry. But that reminds me: Is this what you were looking for in the hall yesterday?" She showed him the library book. "I found it, vacuuming. It was under the umbrella stand."

"Oh, this." Mr. Finch was flustered. "Yes, as a matter of fact, it is. Peter was asking me about volcanoes and I thought he'd be interested to study up on it, so I got it from the town library."

"Good!" Mrs. Finch said. "Peter can take care of volcanoes, and I'll trust you to take care of the furnace."

Mr. Finch dreaded the day when his wife should find out that his calling the furnace a volcano was no joke. It might be only a little one, as Ambrose Marveldale had said, but a volcano is a volcano, and this thing in the cellar was the business end of one.

8

After supper about a week later, Mr. Finch stood on the cellar stairs with Peter, discussing what they had learned from the book.

They looked at their little volcano with new respect, now that they understood what was out of sight underneath the part they could see. Peter advised a drastic treatment.

"Pour a pail of cold water into the nozzle," he said. "That ought to cool it off!"

"That would settle our problems, all right," said his father, "and would probably be the end of Ashfield too. It would blow up before you could say 'Vesuvius.' Don't you know what happens when cold water hits something red-hot?"

"How about warm water, then? Mix cement with warm water," Peter suggested, "and pour it in. Wouldn't that plug it up pretty tight?"

"How would the steam get out?" asked Mr. Finch.

"It wouldn't. That's the idea. The concrete would hold it in."

"And after a good lot of steam pressure was built up inside, then what?"

"Pow!" said Peter. "I forgot about that. Well, if we can't drown it out or hold it in, at least we can rig up an alarm to warn us if it gets too hot or starts to squirt."

"A whistle in the top?" chuckled Mr. Finch. "That was your first idea. Remember?"

Peter blushed. "But seriously, Dad, why not have something that would burn and break if the volcano got hotter than usual? Then something else would drop with a loud bang. I know — we could string a cord across where the steam comes out, and run it through pulleys upstairs to the living room, with a weight on the end, hanging over the punch bowl. And have another weight or something hanging over your bed, to bump you and wake you up in case it dropped during the night."

Mr. Finch thought this a good plan. At least, he could think of no better one. None of his teachers at school when he was a boy had told him how to live safely in a house with a volcano in the cellar.

"It sounds as if we'd have a thermostat on our little monster, after all," he said. "Not to turn it on and off, but at least to sound an alarm." So he gave Peter permission to go ahead the next afternoon after school, and see what he could rig.

"But be careful," he warned, "not to let your mother or Patsy guess what you're doing. And please," he added, "I don't care what you hang over me — so long as it doesn't knock me out — but please don't hang anything over the punch bowl. Try to find something not so precious to make your crash."

For Peter, the next day, school was pretty dull. The clock hands crawled. But the minute he got home, time began to fly. On the way, he had stopped at the hardware store and bought some small pulleys with money his father had given him.

With these, and an old clothesline Mrs. Finch found for him, he went down in the cellar and got to work.

"Don't stir up the dust," his mother called down the stairs. "I wish your father hadn't said you could go down there alone. Since he did, I suppose it's all right. But do be careful."

"Careful!" Peter thought. He looked at the volcano and tried to picture his mother's face if she should see it. Then he tied one end of the cord to a hook at the other side of the cellar, stretched it across directly above the volcano, and passed it through a pulley near the stairs. With the help of two more pulleys, he ran the cord up into the kitchen through the crack over the door, across the kitchen, and into the dining room. There was a swinging door between the two rooms, and Peter puzzled for some time over how to get the alarm cord through. Finally he said to his mother:

"We can keep this door open, can't we? Because if we can't, Daddy'll have to drill a hole here right above it for the cord to go through."

"Mercy on us!" cried Mrs. Finch. "Don't drill any holes. Whatever are you up to, anyway, with all these pulleys and rope? Is it some kind of trap?"

"You better ask Daddy," Peter replied. "I'm not supposed to say what it's for, except — it's a sort of thermostat."

"Whoever heard of a thermos trap?" said Patsy scornfully. "I'll bet it's a ghost trap."

Finally, Mrs. Finch gave permission to run the cord through the opened door. She felt sure he would lose interest in the contraption and take it down in a day

or two, and she thought she could stand the open door and the rope for that long.

Peter made a Y at the end of the cord, one branch leading to a silent alarm in his parents' bedroom and the other to a noisy one in the living room. The silent alarm was a plastic bag full of water, suspended over his father's side of the double bed.

"Wait till Daddy sees that!" Patsy said. "Will you ever get a licking!"

"He said I could," Peter replied grimly. "In fact, he told me to. So there!"

"But what if the string breaks?" Patsy persisted.

"That's the whole point, silly," said Peter. "He wants to be waked up if — " He stopped just in time.

"If what?"

But Peter wouldn't say another word.

The noisy alarm was harder to make. Breaking the glass punch bowl was forbidden, Mr. Finch had said.

But perhaps something smaller could be smashed. At last Peter invented a combination noisemaker — a cluster of objects, some of which would break and other clang or bang. He hung this cluster on the cord in one corner of the living room, as high as he could reach above the floor. There were four old chipped cups, an enamel coffeepot with marbles in it, two burned-out light bulbs, and a piece of steel pipe about three feet long.

Among these articles, to make sure they were heavy enough, and would come down hard if the cord were burned through by the volcano, he hung an old pair of andirons, from an upstairs fireplace where they wouldn't be missed.

Finally he wet a cake of soap and rubbed some on the cord near every pulley, to make it run easily. When he was all done, he took a last look at the cord where it crossed above the volcano. There was no sign that the heat was charring it, yet it was placed just where any flame would burn through it quickly and release the two alarms.

He was still admiring the contrivance when he heard his mother open the kitchen door.

"Yes, perhaps we do need some," she was saying to a man in gray overalls, as Peter reentered the kitchen. "Mr. Finch hasn't mentioned it, but I know the oil tank hasn't been filled since we moved in."

"I'll look, ma'am," said the man at the door.

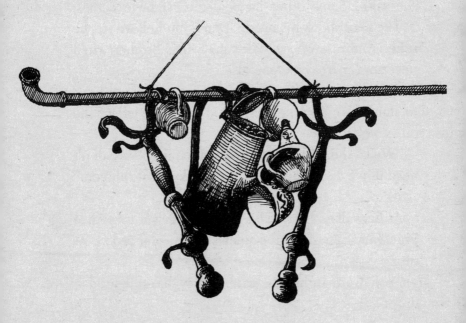

"There's a gauge outside here on the pipe where we fill it." He disappeared for a moment. When he came back, he had a puzzled frown on his face.

"It's almost full," he said. "I can't understand it. When Mrs. Jarvis was here, I had to deliver oil every month right through the winter."

"Well, then," put in Mrs. Finch, "we are probably using what was left over when the Jarvises moved away."

"Couldn't be," the man objected. "There was heat in this house all last winter after they left. And this fall, before you moved in. I haven't filled the tank for over a year."

Mrs. Finch laughed. "It's probably very simple," she said. "Some other oil dealer must have come."

The man shook his head. "Don't you believe it," he said. "Ambrose Marveldale's my wife's brother. He'd never order from anyone else."

Mrs. Finch was beginning to be annoyed, to have to stand here arguing. What did it matter where the oil came from?

"Well," she said, "thank you for coming. If we don't need it, we don't need it. When we do, we'll call you."

As he walked back to his truck, the driver met Alice Pratt hurrying along the sidewalk. She glanced up at him.

"You were right," he said. "They haven't used a drop."

9

"Margaret," said Mr. Finch to his wife one morning as he was getting ready to leave for work, "don't you think the time has come to invite my boss to dinner?"

Mrs. Finch was proud of her cooking and proud of her husband and children. She always expected something awful to happen when important people came to meals, but she enjoyed showing off her family and her skill with food so much that when Mr. Finch suggested something like this, she couldn't say no.

So Mr. Pringle, the head of the baby powder factory, and his wife were invited for a Friday evening two weeks ahead, and Mrs. Finch began making plans.

April had come. Ashfield had lost its snow, all but

the last dirty remnants of it, and the robins that had hopped around Number Seven, Pride Street, all winter long were now venturing onto neighboring lawns. In other houses, the furnaces were idle most of the day. But at Number Seven the heat billowed up out of the cellar just as generously as ever.

"Is the thermostat out of order, dear?" Mrs. Finch asked her husband, eyeing Peter's alarm cord. "Are you having trouble with the furnace?" But he only said, "Yes; some." When she suggested getting a repairman to come and look at it, he grumbled, "Can't do that," and went off silently. Apparently he didn't want to talk about it, but she could tell it was on his mind.

The morning of the dinner party was bright and sunny. At breakfast, Mrs. Finch asked Peter to take down his laundry cord where it went into the dining room.

"I must be able to shut the door into the kitchen," she said, "or all the cooking smells will come right through."

"Besides, Peter hasn't caught anything with it yet," Patsy reminded her.

Mr. Finch swirled the last of his coffee in the bottom of his cup and looked at it thoughtfully.

"No," he said, "I don't think we should ask Peter to take it down."

"Not even with company coming?" Mrs. Finch

said. "But it looks so crude and it doesn't seem to be working very well. I hate to have the kitchen sounds and smells go all through the house. And that collection of hardware and crockery hanging in the corner of the living room!"

"No, Margaret," he said. "Especially with company coming, I wouldn't want him to take it down. It's working all right. We can just open some windows to let the cooking smells out. The Pringles won't notice. Don't worry."

But Mrs. Finch did worry. She opened windows — lots of them. The day became warm and as the house grew hotter and hotter she opened more. By the time Mr. Finch came home, all the windows and doors were wide open. In spite of that, the house felt like an oven.

Dinner was delicious, and both Mr. and Mrs. Pringle had second helpings of everything. Mr. Pringle and Mrs. Finch got talking about hay fever, and he told her that was why he had moved his baby powder factory to Ashfield. He had been bothered by hay fever all his life, and this was the only place he had found where he didn't sneeze all summer long. People who came to see him in his old office in New York had begun to say it must be something in the baby powder that made his sneeze. So he just had to move.

It was amazing, Mrs. Pringle remarked to Mr.

Finch, that summer should be coming so early. Mrs. Finch overheard this and asked if the Pringles could recommend a good reliable heating engineer in Ashfield.

In a moment, everyone at the table was talking about how hot it was. The children begged to be allowed to get out a hose and sprinkler on the lawn after dinner and run through the spray in their bathing suits.

Mr. Pringle lighted up a long cigar and sat back in his chair. He said there was a rumor oil had been discovered right in Ashfield. He had been told someone had an oil well in his cellar and was keeping it secret.

Only Mr. Finch was silent, but he too was thinking about heat.

When they moved into the living room after dinner, Mrs. Pringle sat down by an open window. A stiff breeze had come up and was blowing in upon her. She breathed it in delightedly.

"What a charming mobile!" she said. "And how original!"

Mrs. Finch saw that she was looking at Peter's cluster of cups and andirons, which swung a little in the breeze, twirling and making dull bell-like sounds.

"Yes," said Mrs. Finch doubtfully. "Peter made it."

"Not really!" Mrs. Pringle exclaimed. "What wonderful things they learn in school nowadays!"

Mrs. Finch admitted afterwards that it had been a very successful dinner party, in spite of Mr. Pringle's cigar, the open kitchen door, the cords and pulleys, and the heat.

"But, Harry," she pleaded, "this is only April. What will it be like in June? And August? You say that thermostat Peter put up is working all right, but isn't there any way to shut off the heat?"

"I'm afraid there isn't," Mr. Finch replied sadly. "I'm afraid there isn't. This is the price we pay for having so much good warmth in winter."

"Then wouldn't it be better to have the furnace taken out altogether," she said, "and get a new one that can be controlled, like the ones other people have? Maybe a Volcano is cheap to run in cold weather, but it will be the death of us in summer."

"No," Mr. Finch said, "we can't take it out. It's — it's built in. But I've been thinking. . . . If Peter and I put our heads together, perhaps we can figure out a way to funnel some of that extra heat up the chimney."

For several evenings, Mr. Finch and Peter went mysteriously up and down the cellar stairs with yardstick and tape measure, talking to each other in low voices, busy with pencil and paper. Finally, Mr. Finch telephoned the lumberyard and ordered eight hundred firebricks, a large roll of asbestos, and a dozen bags of heat-resistant mortar mix.

When the order was delivered, it made an enormous pile (an enormous mess, Mrs. Finch called it) on the lawn at the back of the house. But Mr. Finch and Peter had agreed that was the most convenient place to put it. Since the cellar hatchway was there, they could carry the materials down without going through the house and making dusty footprints in the kitchen.

They worked on their heat catcher every evening after supper — Mr. Finch in the cellar laying bricks, and Peter outside mixing a little mortar at a time with a hoe, in a flat wooden box.

Whenever Mr. Finch's mortar pail was empty, Peter would fill another and skid it down to him in the old metal play slide they had brought from New Jersey, even though he and Patsy had grown almost too big to slide on it themselves. He rubbed the slide now and then with a piece of waxed paper to make it slippery, and had no trouble at all keeping Mr. Finch supplied with bricks and mortar as fast as he could use them.

Working at it this way each evening and Saturdays, it took them two weeks to build a clumsy but effective flue, through which the heat of the volcano was carried by a sloping tunnel to the chimney. There it made use of the opening to which the now-idle oil furnace had been connected.

They had not attempted to cement the new brickwork to the top of the volcano. Instead, Mr. Finch had built a sort of hood over the volcano, resting on brick posts, high enough up to leave Peter's thermostat undisturbed. They were both well satisfied with the results, for there was no doubt that nearly all the volcano's heat was now carried harmlessly up the chimney and away.

Life at Number Seven, Pride Street, was so much pleasanter that at first nobody noticed there was a new problem: The draft in the chimney was so strong that now all the air around the house rushed continually upwards.

It was worse than a nuisance. Close by the house, rain couldn't reach the ground. The flower beds dried up and Mrs. Finch had to pour water on them from a pail. When Peter mowed the lawn, the grass clippings flew up into his eyes. Paper napkins were sucked out the dining room windows and blown sky-high, until the family learned never to let go of them.

When Alice Pratt came, about the end of May, to call on Mrs. Finch again, her little hat with a gauze bird on it flew right off her head and went up, up, up, until it disappeared like a toy balloon. Miss Pratt was so busy holding down her skirt, as she waited on the Finches' doorstep, that she neither felt her hat take off nor saw it sail away, but Patsy — home with a cold — glimpsed it soaring aloft past one of her dormer windows.

This was a very strange house, Patsy thought. And she saw no reason why Peter should know the secret of the cellar, when she didn't. No reason at all.

10

That afternoon, Patsy waited in the hall to catch her father when he came home.

"Guess what, Daddy," she said, as soon as he was inside the door. "Miss Pratt came and her hat jumped right off her head while she was standing on the doorstep. It went straight up in the air. I saw it go. Daddy, why is it always so windy around our house? And why can't I go down in the cellar? You let Peter. Why won't you let me too?"

Mrs. Finch came from the kitchen just in time to save him from Patsy's questions.

"I hear Miss Gossip visited you again today," he said. "What was she after this time?"

"I think she wanted to know why the selectmen are coming to call on you tomorrow," Mrs. Finch said.

"Are they?" said Mr. Finch, surprised.

"Exactly! You didn't know either. I didn't tell her it was news to us. I said if it wasn't something private,

59

she would probably know all about it within a day or two."

Mr. Finch gave a wry smile. "And if it *is* private, I'm sure she'll know even sooner! But why would the selectmen be coming to see me, I wonder?"

Usually, Friday evening was the most carefree of the week for Mr. Finch, because of the holiday the next day. But this one was spoiled. Had someone found out about the volcano? He worried until bedtime. And after that he lay awake, sure that the secret must be out.

What would the selectmen do? Would they punish him? Was there a law against hiding a volcano — or just *having* a volcano — in one's cellar in a thickly settled area like Pride Street? Would Ambrose Marveldale be sent to prison? What about Mrs. Finch and the children — especially Peter, since he knew the secret? The hours dragged past.

He hardly touched his breakfast next morning, and the doorbell rang before he was expecting it. He leaped from the table and went to open the door.

There they were, the three selectmen, Mr. Blurt, Mr. Mound, and Mr. Mumble, all firmly holding their hats, which struggled like rabbits to get away in the brisk upcurrent of air.

"Come in, come in," said Mr. Finch as cordially as he knew how, and hoping they wouldn't notice his agitation. "I heard you were coming to see me. What can I do for you?"

The three selectmen sat down in a row on the sofa and looked at him solemnly.

"There have been rumors," Blurt began — Mr. Finch's heart sank — "that a freak of nature has been discovered in Ashfield. A discovery which would affect the whole future of the town."

"An incredible thing," said Mound.

Mumble added something that Mr. Finch didn't quite catch, but Blurt and Mound nodded as if they had heard and agreed.

"We are sure, Mr. Finch, that you are a public-spirited citizen," Blurt continued, "eager for the best interests of Ashfield." He paused. Mr. Finch hastened to assure the three solemn visitors that he certainly was.

"Of course," Blurt said in a scornful tone, "there are some — "

"Some, yes," said Mound darkly.

"Some," went on Blurt, "who might try to keep a discovery like this to themselves, concealing from their fellow citizens the kind of information which all have a right to know. Surely you, sir, are not one of them." He paused again, and Mr. Finch found all three staring at him more soberly than ever. He pretended not to notice.

"But why have you come to me?" he asked.

The three selectmen looked at one another, and Mumble again said something inaudible. The others seemed to be agreeing with him. Blurt turned to Mr. Finch.

"The rumor was . . ." he began. "That is, we thought you could tell us something about this rumor, whether it's true or not."

"We preferred to come straight to you," added Mound, "rather than take other — um — steps."

"You must realize," Blurt urged him, "how important it is to get to the bottom of a rumor of this kind before the Bicentennial celebration opens. If it's true, well . . ." He waved his arm in a sweeping gesture, as if to say that anyone knew what the effect would be. Mr. Finch knew well enough, and so, it seemed, did the three on the sofa. Could they see the beads of sweat on his forehead?

"If some nosy newspaper reporter found out," began Mound, "that a citizen of Ashfield had found in his cellar — "

"An unmistakable flow of natural oil," said Blurt —

"Why, what's the matter sir?"

Poor Mr. Finch was sitting there with his eyes and mouth wide open. "Did you say oil?" he asked weakly.

Blurt looked at him sternly. "A man that's able to run his furnace all winter without ever buying a drop of oil ought not to act surprised," he said. "No, Mr. Finch, the cat's out of the bag. We are appealing to you, for the good of Ashfield" ("For the good of Ashfield," chorused the other two) "to share the news of your discovery. Let us make the announcement of it as a great climax to the Bicentennial!"

"Just think of the glorious future of our town," said Mound, and he sat back with eyes half shut and a dreamy smile on his lips.

The other two kept their eyes fixed on Mr. Finch, waiting for his reply.

"I'm sorry," he said finally. "I can't help you. It's

not true. I haven't discovered any oil."

The selectmen gazed at him in complete disbelief.

"Well," said Blurt, "I must say I . . . . Well, sir, we hope you'll think it over for a few days. Perhaps you will change your mind. Come along, boys." And the three took their hats and went away.

The Finches had a busy weekend.

On Saturday afternoon, Mr. Cramp, the school superintendent, dropped in. Although he said he had come to ask how the children were getting along at the Ashfield school, he was soon talking about something else.

"There are rumors oil has been discovered in Ashfield," he said. "Just think what this would mean to us! A town with natural wealth like that could afford the very best of school facilities — a new building, higher salaries for the teachers — everything!"

"How exciting," said Mrs. Finch. "And how lucky the children will be — Peter and Patsy too!"

Mr. Finch agreed they would, but murmured that he doubted that the oil rumor were true.

"It might be, Daddy." Patsy spoke up from her place on the sofa beside him. "Maybe that's the secret you and Peter have in the cellar."

"No, Patsy," he said, "but I wish it were."

Mr. Cramp raised his eyebrows at this, shook his head sadly, and left.

In the evening, Mr. Pringle rang the bell. "Finch,"

he said, "I am passing the word around that A. J. Pringle's Baby Powder is offering a reward to anyone who discovers oil in Ashfield."

"A reward?" said Mr. Finch.

Mr. Pringle looked at him sharply. "Yes, we'll double his salary if he works for us; one thousand dollars if he doesn't. That ought to smoke him out, don't you think?"

"If there *is* any oil, yes," said Mr. Finch.

Mr. Pringle didn't stay long. "Well," he said, "maybe you'll be the lucky man!" As he went out the door, he caught sight of Peter and Patsy sitting in their pajamas on the stairs listening. "Or it might be one of you," he added.

On Sunday afternoon, Mr. Watts, the parson, came. "How goes it, Finch?" he said. "Are you and the family pretty well settled into Ashfield by now, eh?"

"Oh yes," said Mr. Finch. "It's a friendly town, no doubt of that."

"A friendly town, yes. Yes, indeed," the parson said approvingly. "I'm glad to hear you say that. A preacher like myself surely feels it. It might surprise you to know how often people trust me with — tell me their secrets. And really, you know, there's not a one of us but has some sort of burden — something he needs to get off his chest, own up to — confess, if you don't mind the word. And what a relief it is to be able to bring these troubles to a sympathetic ear!"

So they've set the parson on me too, Mr. Finch thought. He smiled. "Then maybe," he suggested, "the man they say has discovered oil in Ashfield will soon be knocking at your door."

The parson sat very still on the edge of his chair. "You think he may? I do hope so. I do indeed. Perhaps at this moment he is resolving to share the discovery with the rest of us."

Parson Watts gazed hopefully at Mr. Finch, who thought he must say something, and finally stammered:

"Yes. If there *is* any oil."

A week passed with no more visitors. Mr. Finch met Selectman Blurt in front of the post office the following Saturday and greeted him warmly, but Blurt gave him a black look and said nothing.

At four o'clock that same afternoon, Mr. Finch was summoned by his doorbell, to find two men on the doorstep. They looked very much alike, with pencils behind their ears and notebooks sticking out of their side pockets.

"Mr. Finch?" said one of them.

"Yes?"

"Fire Department," the man said briefly and unfolded an official-looking paper, which he handed to Mr. Finch. "Inspection. We've had a complaint. Storage of combustibles without a permit. Fire hazard."

With Mr. Finch leading the way, and Peter trailing apprehensively behind them, the inspectors began in Patsy's room and worked their way through the house, opening every door to look inside. When they reached the kitchen and found the cellar door fastened, they pulled out their notebooks and their eyes grew bright with suspense.

"You keep this locked?" they asked.

"Yes. Yes, I do," said Mr. Finch, his fingers shaking as he turned the key. "The stairs are steep and — furnaces are sometimes dangerous. I — " He left the sentence unfinished.

The inspectors made no comment but followed close behind him and Peter down the stairs, with

Patsy on their heels. Why not? she thought. This was her chance. If the cellar wasn't safe when two fire inspectors were in it, it never would be. Even Mrs. Finch, holding a damp dish towel over her nose and mouth, brought up the rear.

In a moment they were all standing at the foot of the stairs — Mr. Finch white as a sheet; Peter, proud to have his ingenious fire alarm system seen by the inspectors; the two inspectors staring in utter bewilderment at the strange object in the middle of the cellar with the brick hood over it and the cord and pulleys; Mrs. Finch and Patsy, sure that this could not possibly be what it looked like, waiting to hear what the inspectors would say. At last one of them found his voice.

"What is that?" he said.

Mr. Finch swallowed. "A — a volcano."

"You're joking," the man said. "People don't have volcanoes in their cellars. Besides, volcanoes are big things — mountains."

"They start small," said Peter.

Mr. Finch frowned at him to keep quiet.

The inspector edged back towards the stairs. He kept his eyes on the volcano, but spoke over his shoulder to his companion.

"What do the regulations say?"

The other man fingered through his notebook.

"Nothing about volcanoes."

"Well, they ought to," the first man said. "Don't

you realize, sir, the danger to your family, living here right on top of it? And to the town?"

"I know," said Mr. Finch, "but we had to. There was no other place we could rent. Peter rigged up an alarm — that's what the pulleys and cord are for — to warn us if it gets too hot, and of course we would try to spread the word before . . . . Anyway, it's been just like that since we came; it never gets any bigger."

It didn't sound very convincing now, even to Mr. Finch. Moreover, the inspectors were already following Mrs. Finch and Patsy hurriedly up the stairs, not waiting to hear the end of his sentence.

By the time Peter and his father had reached the kitchen, the others were almost at the front door.

"Wait!" called out Mr. Finch in desperation. "What are you going to do? Don't go rushing out like that. You'll have the whole street in a panic."

"You may be right," said the inspector who seemed to be in charge. "But we are certainly going straight to the selectmen to report this. That thing could blow us all up at any moment. The town is living on a powder keg! And here you've been hiding it for six months!"

The two inspectors hurried off down the path, leaving Mr. Finch trembling in the doorway. But his woes had only begun.

"Harry," said Mrs. Finch reproachfully, "why didn't you tell me?"

"I did," said Mr. Finch, "only you thought I was

talking about some kind of furnace. After that, I — I just didn't want to get you all upset. You were so happy here, and this was the only place in Ashfield to live. If we had moved away, people might have found out what was wrong, and that would have been the end of Ashfield and the factory and my job. The volcano is so quiet and — well-behaved — I am sure we could get away if we had to."

"Well-behaved!" snorted Mrs. Finch. "Did you ever hear of Pompeii?"

"They didn't have cars to take them away quickly," objected Mr. Finch.

"And their volcano wasn't in the cellar," Mrs. Finch retorted. "Ours is. You must have been out of your mind to let us stay here. But I can tell you one thing, Harry Finch, *I'm* not out of *my* mind and I'm not going to spend another night sleeping on a volcano — not with all the alarms in the world!"

And she ran upstairs and began throwing clothes into suitcases as fast as she knew how.

Mr. Finch saw it was no use trying to change her mind, so he set about emptying his desk in the corner of the living room and packing the contents into an old grocery carton.

Peter and Patsy went to their rooms and gathered all their treasures together, so that nothing important would be left behind. Mrs. Finch called out to them to pack as much as they could and leave everything else in plain sight on their beds. She would finish it for them.

When Patsy couldn't decide what to do next, she discovered she was terribly hungry. She went down to the kitchen and found Peter sitting there, with a long face, munching crackers. She got herself a glass of milk and a handful of crackers and sat down with him.

For a long time neither of them spoke.

"You ought to be ashamed of yourself," Patsy said finally.

Peter said nothing.

"Imagine keeping a volcano in our cellar," she went on, "like some kind of toy. And keeping it secret, as if it was a bag of peanuts, or something!"

Still Peter said nothing.

"We could have all been buried alive in ashes and lava," said Patsy. "And what about Red and Sally and Marcia and Bim? Supposing they were at the pictures and had the roof fall in on them? And Peggy with her broken ankle. She couldn't possibly run fast enough." Patsy paused to eat another cracker. "You ought to be ashamed of yourself," she said again.

"But Daddy promised Mr. Marveldale he wouldn't tell, and I promised Daddy I wouldn't. It hasn't done any harm to anybody, so why should I be ashamed?"

"Because you never know what a volcano's going to do next, that's why."

"But it may be a thousand years before it does anything. Anyway, if it decides to spout, it'll set off the alarm first." Peter's lip trembled. "Now that we're leaving, we'll never know if the alarm works or not."

"Peter!" Mrs. Finch's voice sounded from the hall. "Patsy! Get your coats! We're ready to go."

They found their father and mother standing at the door, surrounded by suitcases and boxes. One of the boxes, with no top, was crammed full of last-minute things — books, neckties, coat hangers, baseball bat, alarm clock. On top, Peter saw the book about volcanoes.

"We must stop at the town library on our way and leave that," Mr. Finch said, when he noticed Peter looking sadly at it. "I'll tell you what though, Pete, I'll get another copy at a bookstore that you can have for your own."

"Are we all ready?" said Mrs. Finch.

"Just one other thing," Mr. Finch remembered. "We ought to phone Ambrose Marveldale."

But while he was looking for the number, a jumble of voices was heard outside and a commanding knock sounded on the door.

12

The door opened before Mrs. Finch could turn the knob. In marched the three selectmen, Mr. Pringle with his cigar, Mr. Cramp, the parson, and the two fire inspectors. They were all out of breath, especially Parson Watts, who leaned against the door jamb with his eyes half closed, taking long breaths.

Selectman Blurt glanced at the pile of luggage in the hall. He held up his hand. "Stop!" he said. "Put down the telephone! We must talk with you at once."

"Now!" echoed Mound.

"Immediately!" said Mumble. And for once he made himself heard.

They paraded into the living room. Peter brought some kitchen chairs, and the callers sat down in a row on one side of the room, facing Mr. and Mrs. Finch and Peter and Patsy, who sat on the other side.

Blurt drew a deep breath. "Cooke and Cabot, here" — he pointed at the two inspectors — "have brought us shocking news. In all my years as superintendent

73

of streets, assessor, and selectman in Ashfield, a town noted for its architectural charm and healthful air, I never thought a thing like this could happen — that respectable citizens should be found to have a — a" — he dropped his voice — "a volcano in their cellar."

"On one of our finest streets too," put in Mound, in tones of deep dismay.

"And on the eve of the Bicentennial!" added Pringle. He clamped the cigar tightly between his lips.

Mr. Finch and Peter looked at the floor. Patsy blushed crimson. Mrs. Finch nodded her full agreement with what the visitors had said. Parson Watts cleared his throat.

"We must not be unduly harsh," he said. "It is plain to see that these good people are full of remorse. I am sure they are eager for a chance to atone, to cooperate now with us for the welfare of the community."

"Oh yes, we are indeed," exclaimed Mr. Finch, relieved by this sign of forgiveness. "But what can we do?"

Blurt, Mound, and Mumble glanced at one another and at the men who had come with them. It seemed that Blurt was to be spokesman for them all.

"Since you wish to be helpful," he said, "our task is easier. Parson Watts is absolutely right: We don't want to be harsh. I don't know but what any one of us might have had the misfortune to find a volcano in his cellar. If it had been me, I can't say for sure that I would have acted any more wisely than you people. But anyway it's happened, and the danger has to be met, head on."

"Yes, but how?" asked Mr. Finch. "Will you tell everybody to move out of town?"

"Not at all! Just the opposite, in fact. We want you people to stay in this house and say nothing about the volcano, for just a little longer."

"Stay in this house!" cried Mrs. Finch.

"Say nothing!" cried Mr. Finch.

"Only for a little while," Blurt repeated. "Only until the Bicentennial is over. To start people worrying about this just now — maybe needlessly — would ruin all our preparations. Nobody would come into Ashfield from out of town. Many of our own people would leave without being asked to. It would be a calamity."

"A disaster for the factory too," groaned Mr. Pringle. "But if the news is delayed a little, we may perhaps find a way to keep going in spite of it."

"Exactly," Blurt agreed. "The only solution we can see is for us in this room — there are just twelve of us — to keep the whole thing secret until after the celebration. Then — "

"But that's not a little while — it's almost two months!" Mrs. Finch broke in.

"And it's dangerous!" exclaimed Patsy, before the selectman could answer.

Mr. Cramp gazed at her severely. "A child," he said, looking down his nose, "might not understand, but the greatest danger to Ashfield now is to lose its good name."

"On the eve of the Bicentennial," added Mr. Pringle.

"And therefore," said Parson Watts, "we must all have the courage to say nothing about it. There is danger, yes, but remember, wherever we live, we live at the Lord's pleasure. There is always danger, everywhere — even in a church."

Mrs. Finch found her voice again. "Then you won't let us leave this house?"

"No ma'am, we can't," replied Blurt. "There was gossip enough when the Jarvises left. If you did the same, the cat would be out of the bag in no time. You wouldn't want to start a panic, would you?"

Mrs. Finch was about to answer when there came a frightening noise from the corner of the room — a crashing, smashing, clanging bim-bam-bang.

"Daddy!" Peter shouted. "The alarm! The alarm! The volcano! It's going to erupt!"

It was like a pocketful of marbles falling through a hole, the way that house emptied out.

In a moment they were all huddled at the curb, staring back fearfully at Number Seven. The house stood with its door wide open, as innocent-looking as ever.

"Now let's not be panicky," said Blurt in a quavering whisper. "Let's not be panicky. We're lucky it's suppertime just now; probably no one has seen us. You said that — that racket was an alarm?"

"It means the volcano's heating up," Peter put in excitedly. "We fixed a thermostat to warn us. And boy, did it ever work!"

"That's right," Mr. Finch assured the others. "There may be smoke or even flame coming out of the chimney at any moment."

They all looked where he pointed, but although they watched for several minutes, no smoke or fire appeared.

"We'd better investigate," said Blurt at last. "Cooke and Cabot, you go in and look around."

But the inspectors hung back.

"Come on, Daddy," Peter spoke up. "Let's go look. We're used to it."

So back into the house they went, stopping every few steps to listen — Peter and Mr. Finch, with the two fire inspectors following unhappily behind.

It was a warm June evening, but the selectmen and Mr. Cramp and Mr. Pringle and Parson Watts and Mrs. Finch and Patsy all were shivering when the brave four came out again to join them. Even Mr. Pringle's cigar was shivering in his mouth.

Mr. Finch chuckled. "It's all right," he said. "Not the end of the world after all, just a mouse. Peter soaped that alarm cord of his where it went through the pulleys, and a mouse gnawed it (for the soap, you know) until it broke, just inside the cellar door where no one noticed. Our little Vesuvius is just as tame as ever. Won't you all come in again?"

But one by one the visitors made excuses for not staying. Instead, they all returned to their separate houses, first securing Mr. and Mrs. Finch's promise to say nothing and to remain at Number Seven, Pride Street.

As he mended the broken cord and rehung the alarm in the living room, Peter thought happily that he had never before shared such a big secret with so many important people.

Mr. and Mrs. Finch were not so happy. They found their bed had been soaked by the bag of water and they had to move to another room. It would be days before their own mattress dried out. Mr. Finch muttered bitter words about the mouse as he went around setting traps, and Mrs. Finch almost agreed with him. If they were going to have their bed drenched again, it had better be the volcano that did it.

But Patsy had made no promises. She still didn't think a volcano in the middle of town ought to be hushed up. And that night before going to sleep she determined to find a way to warn Ashfield.

The warm days passed one by one. School let out. July came. And the Fourth of July. But this year the people of Ashfield were not so excited about the Fourth as usual: They were looking ahead to the greater celebration that would fill the last two weeks of the month.

The evenings were long, and even on the hottest days there was a pleasant breeze. Never did the older citizens of Ashfield remember a summer so comfortable. From all sides of town, it seemed, breezes blew inward towards Pride Street, and when they reached Number Seven they turned and rushed straight up, carrying heat and dust and every kind of worry away into the blue sky.

Even Patsy lost some of her worry about the volcano, though she never quite forgot it. During the first few days, she had expected to hear it rumbling at any moment. She pictured herself running from house to house, hammering on the doors with her fists, to warn the neighbors to flee.

But a week passed, two weeks, three weeks, and nothing happened. There were days now when she nearly believed it had all been a dream. Life was full of fun and games, and Ashfield seemed the best place in the world.

Peter discovered his kite would go higher and faster over Number Seven, Pride Street, than anywhere he had flown it in his life before. It felt as if something up there was pulling on it, like a huge invisible puppy with its legs braced, tugging on a rope.

Peter invited his friends over, and before long every boy and girl in town had heard that the front lawn of the Finches' house was a kite-flying heaven. On sunny afternoons, passersby would see the kite flyers standing all around the edge of the lawn, as their bright-colored paper diamonds, boxes, dragons, and shields — lashing paper tails — tugged higher and higher over the Finches' chimney.

Parson Watts had no intention of giving away the secret, but he did preach solemnly to his congregation about the dangers and uncertainties of life. He would have felt guilty not to warn them. "If they only knew!" he thought. The trouble was, they didn't; they had heard him preach so often about the lurking perils of life that the quavering of his voice now only made them smile. He mentioned earthquake, fire, and flood; wild beasts, vipers, volcanoes — what more could he say? At least, he told himself, he had fulfilled his duty to warn the congregation in a general way, but without upsetting them. After that, his own shock and alarm wore off. Life in Ashfield seemed to him once more about as pleasant and permanent as life could be.

The selectmen also relaxed — but first they wrote a letter to their congressman marked *Private and Urgent: to be opened by Congressman Wherry only.*

Ashfield, they told him, was in danger of being wiped out. Would he please use his influence to get government help to seal up the volcano before it grew bigger? And was he remembering his promise to be present at the fireworks display on the last day of July?

The congressman's reply, written in pen and ink, came by registered mail. He was very sorry to hear about Ashfield's volcano. Although he would inquire at the Department of the Interior, he doubted if there were any way to plug a volcano. Meanwhile, he said, he agreed with the selectmen that not a word about it must be allowed to leak out:

If the people of Ashfield once become alarmed and start to move away, the panic will quickly spread to the rest of Ash County. In no time, the district will be empty — no people, no industry, nothing. Of course, that would be the end of my position in Congress, and who would you write to then if you had a problem like this one? Besides, the volcano may not erupt for years. So stand fast! Have courage!

The congressman added a note at the end of his letter:

Did I promise to come to Ashfield on July 31? I am very much afraid I shall be unable to leave Washington after all.

Next day, another handwritten letter came from the congressman:

I hope you understand that I am just as concerned about your future as about my own career, when I say this matter must be kept secret.

If any rumor of it gets out, I will bring you into court for disturbing the peace. Think of it! All those thousands of people going about their peaceful affairs, over many hundred square miles — it would be criminal to throw them into a panic with such an outlandish piece of news. Your terms in prison would undoubtedly be long. So take care!

The Department of the Interior informs me there have been no volcanoes in my district for millions of years. I asked them if it was possible for one to appear there now. They said nothing was impossible, but they couldn't imagine anything unlikelier.

This being so, I think we might agree the whole thing is a package of ridiculous gossip, without a word of truth in it.

Sincerely, your friend,
Clifford P. Wherry

P.S. Destroy this letter after you have read it; also yesterday's.

The selectmen found Congressman Wherry's argument persuasive. When they considered, also, that years might pass before the volcano erupted, it did seem foolish to worry about it. Look at all the people of Ashfield absorbed in their daily tasks and pleasures! Why upset them over something that might not be dangerous after all?

Mr. Pringle praised the selectmen for this commonsense view of the matter.

"Ashfield has never been so well off," he said. "The factory is bringing all sorts of business to town; employment is high. We can afford to run a small risk.

Personally, I think that report of Cooke's and Cabot's may have been greatly exaggerated. What do they know about volcanoes? Have they ever seen one?"

From the kitchen of Number Seven, Pride Street, everything looked very different, very simple. Behind that locked cellar door was a real live volcano. Mrs. Finch kept pausing to listen as she made meals for the family. Many nights, she tossed and turned in bed. Her husband tried to reassure her.

"After all, it's not a whole volcano," he said. "It's only the nozzle."

Mrs. Finch snorted. "If a tiger stuck his head through the window, I suppose you'd say, 'It's only the teeth.'"

The fact was that Mr. Finch was more concerned about the volcano than he pretended to be. For several days he had noticed wisps of steam at the top of the chimney. This was something new. Did it mean the tiger in the cellar was getting ready to roar?

14

The Chief of Police had never seen so many cars. Since the opening of the Bicentennial, his arms had ached all night from the wigwagging exercise of directing traffic all day.

Many people had arrived the first day and settled down to stay for the whole two weeks. But like the July breezes, carloads of visitors continued to pour into Ashfield from north, south, east, and west.

"Let them park on the sidewalks; let them use the village green," Selectman Blurt told the chief. "After all, it's only once in two hundred years! There'll be plenty of time to clean up after they've gone."

Sneezers' Rest, the rickety old Ashfield Inn, had been reopened for the occasion, scrubbed and painted, its lawn cut, and its drive weeded and raked. Of course, it was nowhere near large enough for all the overnight visitors. The others were made welcome in spare rooms rented by the villagers of Ashfield and in a temporary trailer town set up by an enterprising businessman on the outskirts beyond the baseball field.

At the soda fountain, Mr. Bemis scooped four hundred sixty-seven ice-cream cones on the fourth day — more than were usually sold in a month — and ran out of vanilla. When an ice-cream truck from Hampton drove into town with a fresh supply and became jammed in traffic three blocks from the drugstore, Peter and some of his friends volunteered to carry the cartons the rest of the way, slung on poles between them. Mr. Bemis was so grateful that he got out a double cone for each of them and let them choose their own flavors.

In the midst of this emergency, Selectman Blurt had a bad scare when he looked out the Town Hall window and saw clouds of steam rising from the street among the stalled cars.

Could it be — ? But when he arrived on the scene, panting and muttering to himself, "It mustn't be, it mustn't be," he found the steam was all coming from a chunk of dry ice that had fallen from the back of the ice-cream truck.

Mr. Tunn, who owned the beer parlor, let it be

known that out in Indian Acre, a weedy meadow belonging to him on the edge of town, he had dropped half a dozen arrowheads. To the lucky finders of these trophies, he would supply free beer for the remainder of the two weeks (free popsicles or milk to children). A ticket to hunt for an hour was given to anyone who spent a dollar or more at his bar or snack counter. Not many Ashfield people joined the hunt. Indian Acre had a bad reputation: It was the one place in town which could send the hay-fever sufferers into fits of sneezing. But so many strangers accepted Mr. Tunn's challenge that by the fifth day he had handed out something like a hundred eighty-five tickets. So far, not a single arrowhead had been found.

Jolly Mr. Tunn did relent and give a free beer to the man who found a little hat with a gauze bird on it hanging on a bush in Indian Acre. If it wasn't an arrowhead, Mr. Tunn said, it was certainly some kind of antique, and he wore it perched on his bald head every day after that, as he worked behind the bar.

Patsy saw it on him and knew right off it was the same hat she had watched flying into the sky past her dormer window two months before. But when she told her mother, Mrs. Finch said Alice Pratt would probably be just as happy *not* to hear that Mr. Tunn was wearing her hat.

One of the attractions which had brought many

people to the Ashfield Bicentennial was the series of historical entertainments performed in the evenings at the baseball field.

Some of these were pageants with bright costumes and music and solemn action, like the first one, which depicted The Granting of the Charter to Sir Alpheus Pride by King George the Second.

Some were comic, such as the reenactment of President Grant's famous picnic on the veranda of Sneezers' Rest (including the horse that ate the President's lettuce sandwiches) or The Ashfield Daylight Savings Rebellion of 1926.

There were suspense and thrills enough to suit anybody in the performance on the thirteenth evening — The Burning of the Ashfield Stockade by Chief Wegoduit. The fire truck stood by, out of sight behind the bleachers, with hose ready, as flames shot twenty feet high above the blazing "stockade" and high school senior boys dressed up as Indians danced in and out of the smoke, yelling and whooping.

A Mrs. Winkle from Sheffield, Massachusetts, who was expecting a baby in September, had to be hustled off between the scenes to the Ash County Hospital, where she gave birth to twins while the coals of the "stockade" were still red.

Everyone agreed that the Ashfield Bicentennial was turning out to be a great success. Even Mrs.

Finch had mostly forgotten her fears and was hard at work with the committee of ladies who were to guide visitors on a tour of historic houses on the last day.

But in all the bustle there were two people whose thoughts were busy with other things.

One was Mr. Finch. He had noticed lately a little more steam each day at the chimney top. He was sure, too, that the cellar was now hotter than it had been when the heat flue was first built, even though Peter's alarm cord looked as solid as ever. He shared his misgivings with no one, but he told himself that as soon as the celebration was over he must warn the town.

The other person was Patsy. On the twelfth morning she had wakened to find herself covered with little red spots. Her head ached and she felt miserable. "Chicken pox," said the doctor.

"What?" said Mrs. Finch. "In July?"

"I know," the doctor said. "You're right, it's unusual. But that's what Patsy's got. All those strangers in town, I suppose. Keep her in for about three weeks."

So poor Patsy was left at home while everyone else was out enjoying the last days of celebration. By the next evening, she was feeling much better, except for an unpleasant roaring in her ears. Or could the sound be coming from the chimney? She put an ear against the bricks. There was a roaring like wind, which she had never heard before.

Perhaps the volcano was heating up. What if an eruption began while the crowds were still in town? While the streets were jammed with cars? Only a few, Patsy was sure, would be able to escape. Someone, somehow, must warn them while there was time. But her parents had promised to say nothing. She must do it herself, and without their knowledge.

It was now the thirteenth evening, and Patsy could see from her window the glow of the fire at the baseball field, as the "Indians" destroyed the "stockade." Soon her parents and Peter would be coming home for the night. But tomorrow there would be a chance to slip out and spread the alarm. Even if she still had spots, she would have to do it then. Maybe Peter would help.

It would be better for Ashfield to catch chicken pox than be buried in lava!

15

In the morning, Ashfield was a strange sight. People who waked early and looked out the window rubbed their eyes and pinched themselves. Snow? It couldn't be. Yet it did look like snow. On all the roofs and doorsteps, up and down every street, on everybody's lawns and trees and bushes lay a thin white coating.

The selectmen soon found out what it was, and Mound and Mumble were out before breakfast hiring crews of youngsters with brooms to clear it away. It was ash.

Selectman Blurt stayed at the telephone. "Yes, yes," he repeated to the scores of people who called, "it's nothing to be alarmed about. Simply some ashes from the performance at the baseball field last evening. It was windy later and they blew all over town."

But Blurt knew better, especially after Mumble informed him that by ten o'clock four dump-truck loads of swept-up ash had been removed from the sidewalks alone.

"Four loads!" said Mumble. "And not like any ashes I ever saw before."

Luckily, Mr. Pringle offered his two trucks from the factory to help with the job, because the sweepers were making piles of ash faster than the town's own trucks could carry them away.

"That wretched volcano," muttered Blurt. "Will it spoil the last day of the Bicentennial, after keeping quiet up till now?"

Mr. Finch had slept soundly. The water-bag alarm had not dropped on him during the night, but about six o'clock he had been aroused by someone gently shaking his shoulder. It was Peter.

"Hey, Dad," Peter whispered. "Wake up! There's ash on the grass all around the house."

Mr. Finch slipped out of bed and dressed quickly. He found Peter waiting for him, already dressed, at the top of the stairs. They tiptoed down and out the kitchen door and looked up at the chimney.

Mr. Finch had no idea what they might see — certainly something worse than steam.

Strange to say, however, the chimney top this

morning showed not a wisp of steam, nor of anything else, either. In fact, nothing; and the wind was no longer blowing upwards around the house.

Patsy had slept so much the day before that she woke as early as anyone. From her lookout windows, she saw the strange white blanket covering the town; and then she saw Peter and Mr. Finch go out and look up at the chimney. Whatever had happened, they must be thinking the volcano was to blame.

Soon she saw Peter run out with a broom to join the squad of sweepers who were coming down Pride Street eight abreast, sweeping the ash before them. At half past eight her father drove off to work at the factory, and, last of all, out went Mrs. Finch at five minutes to nine, looking very businesslike with a yellow Bicentennial Guide tag in her buttonhole.

Patsy waited till her mother disappeared around the corner onto Main Street.

"Now," she said to herself, "here I go, spotty or not."

There was no need to tiptoe because everyone else had gone out, so she ran downstairs, jumped the last two steps and hit the front hall floor with a thump.

Out of the kitchen came Peter, a sandwich half in his hand, half in his mouth. They stared at each other.

"I thought you were sweeping," Patsy said.

"All done," Peter explained briefly, between bites. "Now I'm having breakfast. I thought you were upstairs in bed."

"Peter — what's that white stuff?"

"On the street?"

Patsy nodded. "And all over everything."

"Ashes."

"They came from our volcano, didn't they?"

"They might've."

"I think they must have."

"Maybe," Peter said, and licked some peanut butter off his fingers.

"Or maybe you think all those ashes came from Mr. Pringle's cigar!"

Peter frowned at his sister. "You ought to be in bed," he said. "Daddy and I are taking care of the volcano. You're supposed to be taking care of your chicken pox."

"Pooh to chicken pox, and pooh pooh to you and Daddy," said Patsy, "if you let the volcano blow ashes all over town. I don't call that taking very good care of it."

Peter laughed. "I suppose you could have stopped it?"

"No, and you can't either. But there *is* something we can do. We can warn people."

"Not after promising Mr. Blurt we wouldn't," Peter reminded her.

"I didn't promise," Patsy said, "and you didn't either, did you? It was only Mummy and Daddy. Why can't we go out right now and tell people? We could go to the neighbors and our friends, and — "

"Didn't you hear what Mr. Blurt said? It would start a panic."

Patsy wrinkled her nose. "What's a panic?" she asked.

"It's like if — " Peter began. "It's like if somebody sits down on a yellow-jacket nest at a picnic. When people have a panic they get so scared they act crazy."

"Will we have a panic when the volcano erupts?" Patsy said. "That'll be worse than yellow jackets."

"Gosh, yes," Peter agreed.

"And lots of people won't have time to get away."

"No, I guess not."

"Then if we're going to have a panic anyway," Patsy said triumphantly, "why can't we have it right now? We can tell everybody about the volcano, and they can have their panic, and then they can escape before the volcano erupts."

Instead of answering Patsy's question, Peter asked one of his own. "Who says the volcano's going to erupt?"

Back and forth they argued it. Several times Peter was almost ready to tell Patsy she was right, but then he didn't see how she could be. If she was, then Mr. and Mrs. Finch and the selectmen and Mr. Pringle and Mr. Cramp and the parson and the fire inspectors would all have to be wrong. Besides, Patsy couldn't answer his question. Whenever he asked how she was so sure the volcano would erupt, all she could say was, "Well, it might," or "How do you know it won't?"

Before they knew it, the morning was gone. Peter caught sight of Mrs. Finch coming home for lunch and Patsy dashed upstairs to her room. Mrs. Finch found her in her bed a few minutes later, reading a book and looking just as if she'd been there all morning.

Patsy's heart jumped when her mother asked if she would mind being left alone again all afternoon. There would be no more tours of historic houses; instead, the tour committee was going to help decorate the stands at the baseball field for the final evening performance of fireworks and she had asked Peter to go along with her. At last — the opportunity Patsy had been waiting for!

Soon after lunch, Mrs. Finch and Peter left her alone again, and at about two o'clock Patsy slipped from the house unnoticed and made her way by back streets towards the center of town.

16

Patsy had reached the fire station before she stopped to wonder whom she would tell first about the volcano. So far, she had met no one she knew. There were hundreds of strangers. She might look for her school friends — but where?

No use to go to the town officials. They would probably lock her in the jail if they knew she intended to give an alarm.

Perhaps some other grown-ups might help. Mr. Starch, the librarian — he was always asking her what she was reading and thinking about — surely he would listen!

Calvin Starch was alone in the library. While most

of Ashfield was busy encouraging the visitors to spend as much money as possible in town before the celebration ended, it pleased him to make no charge for the exhibits of Ashfield history set up in the library. Yet no more than a handful of people had bothered to come to see them.

"Mr. Starch! Mr. Starch!" cried Patsy. "Do you know anything about volcanoes?"

"A little. What, particularly, do you mean?"

"I mean, do you know anything about volcanoes around here — in this town?"

"Volcanoes in Ashfield? Well, not lately, Patsy. But this part of the country did have many volcanoes long ago. That's how the town got its name. The first settlers discovered the soil here was very fertile, being full of chemicals from the ash of those old eruptions. We have a good book about volcanoes — I think your brother Peter was reading it. Would you like to see it?"

Patsy said, "No, I —" and stopped. How could she tell him? What should she say?

"I came to let you know," she began, "everybody ought to know, we may have an eruption here any time. And a panic. We could be buried like Pompeii."

Calvin Starch smiled. "Don't let it worry you, Patsy," he said. "If volcanoes ever become active again hereabouts, there will be plenty of warning. You haven't seen one, by any chance, on the lawn or in your cellar, have you?"

He gave her a friendly smile and Patsy found she simply couldn't say, "Yes." It sounded too silly. But she couldn't say, "No," either.

"Maybe," she said.

"Better put a cork in it, then, until the Bicentennial's over," he laughed. "They won't want any fireworks like that interfering with the big program tonight!"

Patsy roamed the streets for two hours. But everybody was either too busy to listen to her or too used to the Bicentennial's marvelous events to pay attention to what she said.

A big dump truck rumbled past her soon after she left the library and a group of boys coming towards her on the sidewalk pointed at it and jeered. In the truck was a smooth white mountain of ash, swept up from the streets. On the driver's door was lettered: A. J. PRINGLE'S BABY POWDER.

"Yay, Pringle Powder!" the boys yelled. "Sell it by the ton!"

Patsy passed them with her eyes on the ground. They would only laugh if she warned them of a volcano in Ashfield.

She met Mrs. Watts, the minister's mother, on the sidewalk near the church, and tried to tell her. Mrs. Watts was a kind old soul who loved children, but she was very deaf.

"Mercy on us!" she exclaimed. "A volcano! How exciting! What will they think of next? I must certainly go to the fireworks if there's to be a real volcano too. I'm so glad you told me, dear."

It was hopeless. Patsy went disconsolately home, so as to be there before the others came back for supper. How could people be so stupid? Did they have to have a mountain fall on them before they would listen to a warning? No wonder the people of Pompeii were buried by Vesuvius. It would be just the same in Ashfield. Patsy burst into tears.

She was still lying face down on her bed when Mrs. Finch brought her supper. Red-eyed, she sat up and began to poke at her food without saying a word.

Mrs. Finch was sympathetic. "Patsy, dear," she said, "I know how you feel, missing it all. Wouldn't you like to have one of us stay home with you this evening? I don't really need to go to the fireworks. Let me stay here with you."

"Oh, no, Mummy," Patsy said. "Don't do that. I'll be all right. And anyway, the fireworks that go up in the air I can see from my windows."

Patsy didn't want company. She had been making her own plan for the evening — one more attempt to warn the town. When all the people were together at the fireworks, she would have a perfect opportunity.

Supper was over. Mr. and Mrs. Finch and Peter started off for the baseball field. The clock said seven-thirty. The performance would begin in half an hour.

Patsy's plan was to arrive about half past eight, when everyone was there. But her disappointing afternoon had left her more tired than she realized. As she sat waiting alone in the big quiet house for the hands of the clock to move around, her eyes closed, her head nodded, and she fell asleep.

There came a sudden thudding sound from the cellar.

Patsy jumped awake. What was that? The house was still shaking a little. There was a dull, distant rumbling. The clock said five minutes past nine.

Her heart racing, Patsy rushed out the door as fast as she could go.

17

Not a person was in sight. At the end of Pride Street, Patsy glanced back over her shoulder, thinking she would see a jet of fire bursting from the chimney of Number Seven. No, it was dark and still. Maybe the eruption wouldn't begin right away. She must get to the baseball field before the crowd started to leave.

She ran without stopping. She had left the last houses behind and was still five minutes from the field when a brilliant white streak shot suddenly up into sight ahead of her. Up, up, up it went and then, *boom*, it exploded into a shower of red stars. She heard the roar of people cheering.

Out of breath, she stood for a moment watching

the red and orange sparks drift slowly down. Then another streak of light shot up, and another and another. Six of them, side by side, arched overhead and Patsy followed them with her eyes until they burst in stars, one after another, falling slowly through the warm night air as if they were sinking in water.

It was a thrilling sight. But Patsy had heard there was to be something really spectacular at the climax; if this was it, that would mean the fireworks might be nearly over.

"Hurry! Hurry!" she muttered to herself. "Hurry!"

Paying no heed to the hiss and boom of fireworks, which now cut and spangled the sky in a continuous gaudy display, Patsy ran on, to the very edge of the baseball field.

The crowd was enormous. Roaring with delight, it not only filled the bleachers at the sides but formed a solid wall around the rest of the field. Only at one end did Patsy see a gap where no onlookers were standing. Through it she could get to the platform with the microphone, where the officials sat.

"Hurry!" she told herself. "Hurry!"

"Hey there! Watch out!" she heard a voice. "You can't go there. That's the way the fireworks are aimed. Nobody allowed beyond those flags!"

A policeman was motioning her back. Oh, why couldn't he be looking the other way? But — he wasn't watching her anymore! He had turned to the people around him. Alarmed voices were crying, *"FIRE! LOOK!"*

The cry spread through the crowd like a rising wind. No one cared about the fireworks now. Their eyes and thoughts were all on Ashfield. Patsy swung around and looked too.

A red glow hung over the town. The volcano! But Patsy heard them shouting it was a *fire*. They didn't know. They were beginning to move to their cars. Hurry! Hurry! She must stop them; keep them from going back into town!

No one saw her race through the gap in the crowd, straight towards the center of the field. Ahead, the fireworks crew was setting off the last burst of the display — a fountain of fire and smoke, out of which sprang tall stems of light, forty, fifty, sixty feet high. Dark figures ran past her from all sides, but Patsy dodged her way to the low platform beyond the fireworks pit.

Up onto the platform she scrambled. There were the selectmen, the chief of police, Mr. Watts, and other men she didn't know, all on their feet, uncertain and alarmed and white-faced in the light of the fireworks. Patsy had never used a microphone before, but she had seen them in pictures and knew what to do.

She seized the upright with both hands to steady

herself and gasped up at the little knob on top, one word, "Stop!" Then again, as loud as she was able, "*STOP! !* It's not a fire — it's a volcano!"

The men on the stand looked at her in horror. She heard the roar of the crowd sink into a low murmur. Had they understood her?

"Volcano!" she cried again. "Volcano!"

The word echoed back from the high wooden scoreboard at the far end of the field. She heard a ripple of agitation from the crowd. Car headlights were flashing on in the parking area. Wouldn't they believe her? "Hurry! Hurry!" her heart cried out. She saw Selectman Blurt coming towards her.

"Volcano!" she gasped again. "It *is.* It's going to erupt. Keep out of town. *LOOK!*" And she pointed towards Ashfield.

The glow over Ashfield was brightening swiftly. In its center there now flared flickers of blue and yellow flame, against which the roofs of the town were like black paper cutouts. There came a roar like distant engines.

Out in the dark crowd, Mr. Finch put one arm around Mrs. Finch and with the other reached for Peter. But Peter was gone — somehow separated from them.

Selectman Blurt had always wanted to be the hero of a crisis. He grasped the microphone from Patsy's hands.

"Fellow citizens and guests," he boomed. "Please stay where you are. Do not return to Ashfield. This is no ordinary fire. There *is* a volcano. The safest thing is to stay here together until morning. If you know of anyone remaining in town, bring the name and location to us at the platform here. We are in continuous touch by two-way radio with the Ashfield fire truck and crew. They will make any rescues that are possible. Parson Watts, will you lead us in singing a hymn?"

The parson was trembling all over. He had never seen an erupting volcano; he had only heard about them. The selectman's request took him by surprise, but somehow he managed to keep his voice steady at the microphone. He seemed so calm that soon the huge crowd was singing along with him almost as cheerfully as boy scouts on a cookout. But no boy scouts ever had so spectacular a bonfire.

18

Peter had slipped away from his mother and father some little time before they noticed him gone. Instead of taking his mind from the volcano in the cellar on Pride Street, the fireworks had only made him think about it more. He had kept looking towards town and remembering Patsy alone on the top floor of the house. Would she know what to do if the alarm went off before they got home?

Sooner than anyone else at the baseball field, Peter saw the red glow appearing over Ashfield. Mr. and Mrs. Finch had their heads tilted back to watch a rocket go up from the fireworks pit. No one was watching him. He slid under his seat feet first, through the open back of the stand, and let himself down to arm's length. It was only a two-foot drop from there, and as soon as his feet hit the grass he was on his way. By the time the crowd was crying, "Fire!" and Patsy was running onto the field, Peter was already at Tunn's Corner on Main Street.

The fire truck roared out of its stall just as he came along the sidewalk. The driver saw him and jammed on his brakes. Three men in black raincoats and firemen's hats were standing on the truck's side platform, gripping the polished brass railing.

"Hey, kid," one of them yelled above the noise of the truck engine, "climb on. Come with us. There's a volcano erupting."

"I can't," Peter called back. "I've got to wake up my sister."

"Who's your sister? Where's she live?"

"Pride Street. Number Seven. Patsy."

"Finch?" the man shouted, and when Peter nodded yes, he reached down a hand for him. "Come along, then — your sister's awake! She's out at the baseball field. She's the one that gave the alarm."

Away went the fire engine through the deserted streets, with Peter and the three firemen on one side, and three more on the other. After each stop to take on a passenger, Peter could hear a scratchy voice on the two-way radio telling them where to go next, and then he had all he could do to hang on, through a wild blur of blowing siren, wind, and lurching speed.

The fire truck made five stops. They picked up a

woman with a very tiny baby from an apartment by the Town Hall, and the policeman on duty out in front; Mr. Nesbit, the manager of Sneezers' Rest; an elderly couple with a parakeet in a cage; and the night watchman at the baby powder factory.

Once, Peter heard a deep rumbling, louder than the engine of the truck. Did the others hear it too? He thought it must be the volcano. But if the firemen heard it, they were too busy finding places on the truck for the new passengers to think much about it.

They squeezed the baby with its mother, and the old lady and the parakeet, in beside the driver. The old man stood on one platform, with a fireman on each side holding him, and the policeman and watchman clung to the ends of the brass rail; Peter and three firemen were on the other platform, and one fireman lay on his stomach on top, gripping the rotating light on the cab in both hands and bracing his big rubber boots against the coils of hose. Mr. Nesbit sat jackknifed in the middle of one of the coils, wedged in like a cork in a bottle.

Finally, the truck headed out of Ashfield as fast as the driver dared go with such a load. When they arrived at the baseball field and drove up beside the platform, the hymn singing changed to cheers. Mr. and Mrs. Finch and Patsy came and hugged Peter and took him to where they had been sitting on the grass behind the bleachers.

They were scarcely seated when, with a bellow like

an angry bull, the volcano unleashed its full power. It sounded as if it might be right there beside them. A few people got to their feet in terror and started to run, but Parson Watts quickly called for more songs — loud ones, like "Old Macdonald" and "The Bear Went Over the Mountain."

When the roar of the erupting volcano threatened to drown their voices, they threw more energy into the songs and sang louder yet. There was no need now for fireworks. The glare from the volcano provided more than enough. Although a strong wind had begun to blow over them towards Ashfield, they could easily feel the monster's heat and were grateful they were not closer.

Before midnight, thick billows of smoke hid the fire of the eruption and covered the whole town, blotting out the lighted windows which the townspeople had left behind them. Was Ashfield in flames? Were rivers of lava rolling like molasses through the streets? No one could tell. But by the rumble and shudder of the air they knew that the volcano was still dreadfully alive.

Sometime after two o'clock in the morning, when voices had given out and many people were dozing, propped against one another in the bleachers or on the ground, Ambrose Marveldale found the Finches. His teeth were chattering so he could hardly talk.

"Please," he whispered, "d-don't tell anyone th-that I knew about this last year. They'd — they'd — I don't know what they'd do to me." He sat down on the damp grass, shivering as if it were October.

Soon afterward, Selectman Blurt came along. Mr. Marveldale hid his face against his knees, hoping the selectman would not recognize him.

"Ambrose," said Blurt quietly, and Mr. Marveldale winced. He could imagine the selectman looking sternly at him in the darkness.

"I hope you will all remember that this — this eruption — is a complete surprise," Blurt continued. "A complete surprise. If the people of Ashfield thought anyone had known about that volcano beforehand and not warned them, they'd run him out of town."

"If there's any town left," said Mr. Finch sadly.

19

Everyone said it was a miracle.

Ashfield had not been destroyed. Not even Number Seven, Pride Street. On the day after the great eruption, the Finches' house stood just as untouched as every other building in town. The people of Ashfield wouldn't have been surprised to discover that they and all their visitors had dreamed together the same unbelievable dream.

But this was no bad dream to be laughed at and forgotten. There had been an eruption, yes, but not in the Finches' cellar after all. When Selectman Blurt and the two fire inspectors made a cautious survey of Ashfield and its surroundings in the morning, they found the volcano had chosen to vent itself in the huge pit of an abandoned granite quarry three miles to the north. A smoking cone of ash and lava some fifty feet high nearly filled the old quarry now. Lava had spilled out at one side, running down the slope towards town, and the fields and hillsides eastward were blanketed white with ash as far as the eye could see.

They found Ashfield marked by hardly any traces of its narrow escape. A few trees had been scorched brown, but most of the great heat had been muffled by clouds of steam that billowed up when red-hot lava reached the shallow water of a swamp lying between the quarry and the nearest houses.

The selectmen were taking no more chances. They forbade anyone to go into Ashfield without special permission until they were sure it was perfectly safe.

From all over the United States, it seemed, supplies came pouring in for the "volcano victims."

There were new potatoes from Maine and early apples from New York, blankets and Band-Aids from the Red Cross, and spinach from New Jersey. The Army Engineers arrived in a procession of brown trucks and set up portable washrooms in the outfield. A vegetable farm in California radioed to one of its big delivery vans not to go to New York City but to go to Ashfield instead; it arrived on the evening after the eruption and unloaded a hundred and forty-four dozen artichokes on first base.

A circus shipped one of its spare tents in a plane

from Florida, with a crew of men to put it up. It covered most of the baseball field and was roomy enough to shelter everybody and everything. Mrs. Finch said the tent smelled of popcorn and she would just as soon get back to Pride Street, but Peter and Patsy and their friends had never had such a picnic in their lives.

They lumped around, two by two, in the Red Cross blankets and pretended to be camels; they divided up into teams of lions and lion tamers and raced in and out of the tent with the lions sometimes in front, escaping, sometimes behind, roaring in pursuit. And when the chief of police told them to quiet down, they marked out big squares in the dusty parts of the ground and played checkers with apples and artichokes.

Congressman Wherry was thankful nobody had been hurt in the eruption, nor any homes destroyed. Nevertheless, it was obviously going to be inconvenient to have a young volcano in his district, so he arranged for a government geologist to be sent to Ashfield to look the situation over and advise what could be done about it.

"Please also inspect the cellar of Number Seven, Pride Street," the congressman said to him. "I have heard rumors of something odd there. Bring me a report, privately, after you've seen it."

The geologist found the quarry-volcano quiet, although still smoking. He told Selectman Blurt the eruption had been a freak. It would probably not happen again in a thousand years. Ashfield, he said, could safely resume its normal life, provided the volcano was kept under close watch, and he suggested that someone be appointed volcano supervisor, to take the volcano's temperature every day and listen for suspicious rumbles in its interior.

Before returning to Washington, he made a quiet visit to Pride Street, where he found the Finches just moving back into their house. Mrs. Finch led him down to see the cellar. He took one look at the volcano and let out a long whistle.

"Is this new?" he asked Mrs. Finch.

"My husband built that chimney thing last May," she said. "And Peter put up all those ropes and pulleys. But the volcano — " She looked at him inquiringly. "*Is* it?" she asked.

"It's a volcano, sure enough," the geologist assured her. "Or it was. How long have you had it in your cellar?"

"Ever since we moved here in December," Mrs. Finch said. "And I think it was here for a while before that."

The geologist shook his head. "Talk about *luck*!" he said. He put on a pair of big asbestos gloves. Then he opened a case he was carrying and took out a long chain with a metal tube dangling on the end. Very carefully he lowered the tube into the hole in the top of the Finches' volcano until the chain went slack in his hand. He fished around with the chain for a few moments.

"Plugged solid at twenty-six feet," he said.

Then he pulled it up again, unscrewed one end of the metal tube, and took out a thermometer. He squinted closely at it.

"Good news," he said. "Only a hundred ninety degrees. You won't need to worry. It's all sealed up down there. Probably happened at the same time as the eruption. And it's nearly finished cooling. If your husband wants to, he can shovel all of this" — he kicked at the small cone of ashes — "back where it came from." He pointed at the hole in the top.

The next day, he made his report to Congressman Wherry. "What you've got up there," he said, "is the very tail end of trouble — not the beginning. But it's unheard of for an area like that, where all the real volcanoes died out ages ago, to work up enough heat for an eruption, so long after. Usually, all you get are little cracks and holes — mofettes and solfataras, we call them — with foul-smelling gas coming out, or steam.

"It's my opinion your volcano will go on smoking for a time and then cool off for good. But have it watched!

"As for that house on Pride Street, they've had a real volcanic vent in the cellar for over a year! Imagine living with something like that in the house and never reporting it!"

Congressman Wherry murmured, "Amazing!" He hoped silently that the selectmen had obeyed his instructions to destroy his two letters.

"Amazing!" he repeated. He handed the geologist a cigar. "I am afraid," he continued, "that the Finches will be bitterly blamed if people in Ashfield hear rumors about that cellar. It would be a great shame, don't you agree?"

"Blamed for what might have happened — yes, I see what you mean," said the geologist.

"Then I suggest you say nothing at all, in your written report, about the cellar of Number Seven, Pride Street."

Since Congressman Wherry was running for reelection in the fall, he mailed to everyone in Ashfield a copy of the geologist's hopeful statement about the quarry-volcano, with a letter telling what he himself had done to arrange for the investigation.

It is a pleasure, the letter began, *to watch over the welfare of the voters of Ash County.* The letter urged the people of the district to pay no heed to any strange rumors concerning the eruption. They would find all the facts in the enclosed report of the government geologist.

Meanwhile, he announced that a medal would be

given to Patsy Finch for her courage and presence of mind in warning the crowd at the baseball field. He planned the ceremony to fall in October, just two weeks before election day. And finally he notified the Ashfield selectmen that he would be on hand to make the presentation to Patsy himself.

20

The great day came. Patsy was excused from school for the morning so that Mrs. Finch would have plenty of time to get her ready — brushing her hair a dozen times and arranging the bow at the back of her new pink dress, and all the rest of it.

One thing worried Patsy. "Will my medal be on a pin, Mummy, or do you think it will be on a ribbon?" she asked.

"Why, I can't imagine," Mrs. Finch said. "Does it matter?"

"I hope it'll be on a ribbon; if it's a pin, he might stick me with it."

School Superintendent Cramp let the other children out at one o'clock and they marched in procession behind the high school band through flag-decked streets to the village green.

There they found the ceremonies almost ready to begin. On the platform, the only stranger was Congressman Wherry, sitting close to the center in a dark suit with a red carnation in his buttonhole. At the congressman's left was Selectman Blurt. Beyond him were Mound and Mumble, and Mr. Pringle from the baby powder factory. At the congressman's right was Patsy, in her new dress and shoes with fancy buckles, and on the other side of her were Parson Watts, Mr. Cramp, and the chief of police. In a row behind them sat the town clerk, the treasurer, the assessors, and the two fire inspectors, Cooke and Cabot.

It seemed to Patsy that the platform must be about a mile high. Sitting there, she could look right over the heads of the townspeople, as well as the scores of visitors from other parts of the county, who were seated below her under the trees on irregular rows of folding chairs. Some leaves had already fallen but they had been raked into neat piles out of the way.

In front, just below the platform, were Mr. and Mrs. Finch and Peter, proudly watching her. She smiled nervously at them.

Patsy had just begun thinking about how it would feel if the medal had a pin and the congressman was clumsy with it, when the clock in the church steeple chimed the half hour.

Selectman Blurt got to his feet and stepped forward.

"Ladies and gentlemen," he began. "Citizens of Ashfield and guests."

Some of the citizens of Ashfield looked at one another and sighed. When he had a platform under his feet and an audience in front of him, Blurt was apt to ramble on and on. Sure enough, the selectman began with a description of the peaceful Ashfield he knew when he was a boy. From there he went on to speak of the town's growing fame as a place where hay fever victims could always find relief, and as a center for winter sports. Then had come the volcano. After that, Selectman Blurt asked, how could their lives ever be the same again?

Congressman Wherry began to fidget. He saw no sense in staying near the volcano any longer than necessary. He wanted to make *his* speech and be off.

But the selectman was not done. He said the people of Ashfield were grateful indeed to their congressman for sending an expert to study the volcano, and happy to know it might never erupt again. The Board of Selectmen, he said, had appointed an inspector of the volcano. They were erecting a sturdy cabin at the edge of the quarry where the inspector would live.

"I am sure," he went on, "there is at least one lad in this audience, alert and courageous, who is already dreaming of becoming volcano inspector for the town of Ashfield in years to come. But that is all in the future. Let us not forget we are gathered here to honor a fellow citizen who, though she may be young in years" (here he turned and bowed to Patsy), "is old in bravery. Ladies and gentlemen, it is a privilege to introduce to you our distinguished congressman, who will personally confer the award. The Honorable Clifford P. Wherry."

The congressman arose, smiled, bowed, and waved to the outer corners of the audience, held up his hand to silence the applause which had greeted him, and began.

For the first half hour of his speech, Patsy thought he was getting ready to pin a medal on himself. He told at length of all that he had done for Ash County, of the obstacles and opposition he had overcome, of his plans for the future welfare of the people of the district. Then for another twenty minutes he spoke particularly of the volcano.

"You may be confident," he said in ringing tones, "yes, Mr. Blurt, you may be confident that so long as Clifford Wherry is safely seated in the House of Representatives in Washington, D.C., no one in Ashfield need worry about living next door to a volcano. I will see to that."

The clock struck three and he had not yet said a word about Patsy. He was still warming up. He beamed at the restless audience.

"You did not come here today," he said, "to hear a political speech. If I have done anything to earn your votes, you will show it on election day. But this afternoon has been set aside to show our gratitude to another — one new in this community who has already served it nobly; one who heard and heeded a warning inner voice which told her of Ashfield's danger — a voice heard by no one else — "

The congressman's face, Patsy noticed, was blushing almost as red as his carnation, but he didn't seem to be sick. His words went rolling on, as strong as ever. "One who — " he was saying.

Would he ever stop? The more he praised her, the less Patsy felt she deserved it. What had she done? The only volcano she knew about — the one at Number Seven, Pride Street — had not erupted after all. The other one, the one at the quarry, had been as great a surprise to her as to everyone else. Why couldn't Congressman Wherry stop talking, give her the medal, and sit down?

Unexpectedly, the congressman turned to her. The audience began to clap. In a sort of daze, Patsy stood up and stepped forward. The sun was in her eyes.

"I don't deserve it," she was saying aloud to herself. "I don't deserve it. I don't deserve it."

"Nonsense, my dear," the congressman was saying to her, "of course you do."

Patsy was close to the microphone now. "But I

don't," she said, and the loudspeakers threw her voice out over the crowd. "I didn't know anything about the volcano in the quarry." She turned to the town officials and dignitaries sitting in a row on the platform. They would back her up. They knew she was telling the truth.

The parson's hands were fluttering against the hymnbook that lay on his lap. Cooke and Cabot had their heads together and were whispering nervously to each other; the three selectmen — Blurt, Mound, and Mumble — sat rigid in their chairs. Patsy thought she had better explain.

"I really didn't," she insisted into the microphone. "You see, it was the volcano in our — "

"There, there, Patsy," Congressman Wherry boomed, "you are a very modest girl. You deserve all the gratitude Ashfield can give."

Then he hung the medal around her neck and began to clap as if the election depended on it.

21

It was a funny thing about grown-ups, Patsy often thought to herself afterwards; they never would listen when you had something important to say to them, and they had queer ideas, too, about what was important.

For instance, why should the selectmen and Parson Watts and the school superintendent and Mr. Pringle and the fire inspectors and Ambrose Marveldale want to come and help her father pour the new concrete cellar floor at Number Seven, Pride Street? There was even a telegram of congratulation from Washington, signed "C. P. Wherry." And Patsy overheard Mr. Blurt telling her father, "Just send the bill to us."

The new floor covered smoothly every trace of the volcano in the Finches' cellar. Mr. Finch took down the firebrick hood he had built and connected the old oil furnace to the chimney again. Peter took down his cords and pulleys, and put back the andirons on the second floor and the enamel coffeepot in the kitchen.

"Now," Patsy said, with a satisfied shake of her hair, "nobody would ever guess we had a volcano. It's all gone."

Peter was downhearted. "I know," he said. "And it was really fun too — having a little one in our own house. There's no secret anymore."

"It's a secret that we *used* to have a volcano."

"Who'd believe that? And what good is a secret when it's something nobody'd believe if you told them?"

Patsy looked surprised.

"What good is it?" she said. "It's a *deep, dark* secret, that's what. It's the safest kind there is."

When Mr. Finch had oil delivered for the furnace in November, the oil man told Alice Pratt, and Alice Pratt passed the word along to everyone she knew. Maybe there wasn't an oil well in the Finches' cellar, after all.

In December, when snow fell, it covered the roof of Number Seven as thickly as it did every other roof on Pride Street, and when the neighbors' roofs were hung with icicles, so was the Finches'. Best of all, the

Finches' robins had gone south with all the rest of the Ashfield birds. And the ground had frozen, and snow was piled outside Peter and Patsy's door in drifts as deep as any their friends' houses could boast.

They built snowmen and igloos and forts. They even made a snow volcano as tall as Peter and splashed water on it, which froze into a hard crust of ice. In the early spring sun, it melted very slowly. When April came, it was the last trace of winter to disappear from Pride Street.